A SHORT TIME TO LIVE

When torrential rain causes a landslide in the remote Lake District village of Sandale it is temporarily cut off from the rest of the world. And this is the splendid background to a tale of blackmail, anonymous letters, conspiracy, a large-scale robbery, kidnapping and murder.

Of course, not all these crimes are the work of the same person, and it's Miss Moffat's well-known amateur detective, Miss Pink, who sorts out the puzzle—but aided this time by the enigmatic Daniel Cole, who claims to be Press but whose interest in Sandale may be more sinister.

Lucy Fell's liaison is notorious. So is Peta Mossop's. Peta's husband, the local innkeeper, deals in stolen property—anything from sheep to loads of whisky. When Peta is murdered and the beautiful Caroline, daughter of newcomer George Harper, disappears, Miss Pink faces a problem which, even by her standards, is extremely complex.

A SHORT TIME
TO LIVE

Gwen Moffat

First published 1976
by
Victor Gollancz Ltd

This edition 2007 by BBC Audiobooks Ltd
published by arrangement with
the author

ISBN 978 1 405 68566 5

British Library Cataloguing in Publication Data available

Printed and bound in Great Britain by
Antony Rowe Ltd., Chippenham, Wiltshire

In this story Sandale and its houses are imaginary, as are all the characters, who have no relation to any specific people, alive or dead.

Chapter 1

I T WAS TWO o'clock on a Thursday afternoon in November and the London-Glasgow express was making good time as it bored through the urban sprawl between Liverpool and Manchester. The fog was thin but it had brought an early dusk to the north country; there were lights here and there in houses, more in offices, and street lamps hung like tangerines in the opal gloom.

The train slipped through a station and past rows of dark brick cottages with outdoor lavatories in grimy yards and lines of nappies limp in the sodden air. In the restaurant car Lucy Fell played with the stem of her wineglass and watched the reflections of her rings in the window. Across the table Denis Noble remarked expansively, 'I should have ordered champagne.'

'We had champagne on the way up.'

'We're celebrating again—aren't we? Going south it was in anticipation of a lovely time, and now we should celebrate an achievement, right?'

She smiled at him and her round and rather large face glowed. The green eyes sparkled and her expression was so infectious that Noble, a ponderous and fleshy man with anxious eyes, looked suddenly boyish and eager.

'All relationships have their ups and downs,' she murmured. 'Thank God we're not humdrum, darling. Chaps are bound to feel their oats sometimes. After all, she was very young. . . .' She returned to contemplation of the interminable terraces, her profile classical in the light. She had good skin and high cheekbones. 'And exciting,' she added.

'You can say that again!' He shifted in his seat. 'And I don't mean it as a compliment. No, Lucy, that's my last oat,

7

I'm afraid; I'm an old man.' He reached across the table and captured her hand. 'You'll have to take care of me from now on.' He caught her expression and his eyes were contrite. 'I know that's a lot to ask after I've made such a fool of myself, not to say hurting you, but at least I've found my level. If I hadn't succumbed to that little tart, I'd have gone on wanting her for the rest of my life.'

She showed no surprise. Her eyes lingered on his thick hair where there was only a suspicion of grey in the black, on the broad face sweating gently after the food and wine, on the wide shoulders and the Savile Row suit.

'You're still a very beautiful woman,' he said. Her eyes slipped as if gear wheels missed a cog. He went on happily, 'And you can still make me madly jealous. You didn't spend much time with me in town but I suppose that was deliberate: wanted to put me in my place, eh?'

'I was shopping.'

'The bills told me that, my sweet.' He smiled to show that no sting was intended and surveyed her costume with interest. She was wearing a silk blouse with a woollen skirt and she'd wound silk scarves round her head. The ensemble, including long suède boots, was in deep shades of green and red and she looked like a German film star playing at being a peasant.

'You don't look a day over thirty, my sweet.'

She shrugged. 'Flatterer.' She fingered the muscles under her jaw where they were starting to slacken. She was forty-four. 'This outfit set me back a packet,' she admitted. 'I'll have to shelve the idea of a Datsun for the time being.'

'Why, how much have you spent?'

'I don't know. About three hundred perhaps.'

'On that!'

'Darling, you like it.' She shot him a glance. 'And *I* paid for this. Besides, there's a cape—and these boots are gorgeous—' Feeling went out of her eyes and left them glacial. She looked at the last of her wine. 'Do I have to justify my spending?' she asked quietly.

8

· 'Of course not. It's just that I like to buy your clothes, you know that.' Her eyes narrowed a fraction. He rattled on: 'I wanted to give you a cheque for the Datsun: to make up the difference when you traded in the Jensen, but I'm not sure whether I can see my way . . . not to both, you know.' Again his eyes went over her outfit and he looked deeply concerned. He wasn't thinking of the cost of clothes nor of the woman wearing them—and she didn't remind him of where he'd been spending his money recently; he was thinking about his business and the state of the economy.

Now it was she who leaned across the table intimately. 'You're going to have a brandy,' she told him. 'Champagne would have been an anti-climax anyway: going home; we'll have a bottle tomorrow night instead. Here's the steward.' She sat back smiling vaguely while Noble saw to the brandy, then she leaned forward again. 'I'll sell a ring,' she said with an air of conspiracy.

He was shocked. 'Those rings are an investment. You're not to sell one to buy something that's going to depreciate. I won't allow it.'

'You didn't give them to me, Denny.'

'But nor would Edward allow you to sell them if he were alive, and he expected me to watch your business affairs, you know that. He said to me, when he knew the end was near—'

'Yes, yes, darling. I won't sell a ring then; I'll sell the bread cupboard, or something. Quentin was suggesting—'

'You haven't told Quentin!'

'Told him what?'

'That you're short of money.'

'Hell, Denny! Everyone's short.'

'Not you; not while I'm alive. You shouldn't have told Quentin about your affairs; what will he—'

The steward came with the brandy. When he'd gone, she said softly, 'Stop bullying me, Denis.'

'You'd set your heart on that Datsun.'

9

'And I've spent it on clothes. That is, I've broken into what I was—'

'How much do you need for the car?'

She licked her lips and looked guilty. He was very red in the face. 'Tell me, Lucy. Five hundred? A thousand?'

'Well, more than five hundred. . . .'

'I don't know whether I could manage a thousand anyway,' he grumbled, reaching for his cheque book, unscrewing the gold cap of his pen. 'Would eight hundred do?'

She nodded. 'It will be ample, darling. You're sweet.'

He signed the cheque and grinned at her, then his face changed. 'What's wrong?' He proffered it abstractedly.

She put it loose in her bag. 'Thank you, darling.' She looked out of the window. 'I was wondering what might be in the post when I get home.'

'Are you worried about something?'

'Not really. Are you?'

'I don't understand. I should be worried about my mail? About the factory, d'you mean?'

'No, I didn't mean the factory.' She sounded a little tired. 'Denny, have you had any anonymous letters?'

He considered the question at its face value. 'Yes, we've had a few: about employees, you know, almost certainly written by other—' He stared at her, astonished. 'You mean, in the dale? *You've* had an anonymous letter?' She nodded, her eyes wide. 'What did it say?' He was grim.

Her face expressed disgust and she tasted her brandy before she answered. 'It was filthy. It accused me of . . . I'm not sure; it was worded so crudely and written by an illiterate. . . . There was something about a baby and burying it in the garden: the garden at *Thornbarrow*! But whether it meant a live baby or a foetus I couldn't say. And I don't care,' she added.

'Nasty.' He was frowning but then his face cleared and he grinned. 'They could hardly accuse me of the same crime.'

'They could—in conjunction.'

10

'I didn't think of that. So you think it's someone who disapproves of us?'

'Well, I wouldn't want to think too much about the kind of person who was compelled to write letters like that.'

'Did you think it was Peta?'

'Peta!' She stared at him. 'This person was illiterate,' she added on a lower note.

'Illiterates can't write.'

'Semi-literate then. Why did you think of Peta as soon as I mentioned it? I never thought—but, of course, she does hate me—and there was that breakdown a few years ago. Poor girl, she really is in love with you, darling, in her fashion. How fortunate you managed to extricate yourself before—well, before any harm was done. You ought to be nice to her when we get back; she could be a bit tricky if she's hostile.'

'If she's writing anonymous letters, I'll avoid her like the plague. She's gone quite haywire, you know.'

'It's not important. I only asked because I wondered if she'd—if you'd had a letter as well and were keeping quiet but were worried all the same. You've got enough on your plate with the factory and—everything.' She shivered. 'Anonymous letters aren't the kind of thing one wants to keep to oneself. The letter doesn't matter, but no one can be easy with that kind of mind living near us, perhaps even in the same dale.'

Chapter 2

AT FIVE O'CLOCK on the day after Lucy Fell returned from London, George Harper glanced across the beck and saw a light in her kitchen window and a faint glimmer in Rumney's cow-house. If she'd started cooking that meant she would have fetched her milk and he didn't have to run into her. He shrugged on his sheepskin, took a torch and the aluminium can and crept down his garden path with caution. The paving stones glistened wickedly and he'd already found to his cost how hazardous slates could be with a veneer of frost.

Sunset lingered above the fells but the dale was black as the pit except for the lights across the beck. Upstream the line of the headwall was humped like a herd of elephants across a fading backcloth and an owl called far out towards Dalehead.

He went down the iron-hard track and crossed the packhorse bridge where the water was unusually subdued; the bogs were frozen above a thousand feet and the level of the streams had dropped.

He came stealthily round Lucy Fell's cottage assessing the stillness in the hamlet. There was no street lamp. Then a bucket rang on stone, a cow coughed, and Rumney's voice came from a byre where the door stood open on a dim interior. The voice was cultured—for the shank-end of a Cumbrian dale.

'Come up there, Isbell; move over.'

' 'Evening, Zeke.' Harper spoke quietly so that he wouldn't alarm the cattle.

Inside the cow-house a hurricane lamp gave as much light

12

as a five-watt bulb. He could just make out the cows' rumps with their incredible hip joints but he couldn't see Zeke, only hear the twin streams of milk as they sang in an empty bucket.

'Good evening.' The disembodied voice came from the direction of the middle cow and Harper moved along and stared at its flank. Now he could just discern the gleam of Rumney's cheek. 'I'm running late,' the voice went on, 'I've been getting the sheep down.'

'I don't mind waiting,' Harper said. 'Have you finished the sheep?'

There was a long pause during which he listened to the cows masticating. Milk started to froth in the bucket.

'Not altogether,' Rumney said at last. 'There's a few missing.'

'Where would they be?'

'Depends.' The milker's face turned to the other but the eyes remained shadowed. The voice continued as if answering an academic question but with the Cumbrian creeping in as it did when Rumney became emotional. 'If they went last night they could still be in t'slaughter-house, but if they be gone longer, they could be in them lyle packets tha picks out of t'freezer in t'supermarket.'

'Oh.' Harper regarded the pale moon-face fixedly. 'Is that kind of thing common round here?'

'Not as tha might call *common*.'

'Have you any idea—? Or don't you like to make a guess?'

'I would prefer to speculate on a certainty,' Rumney said drily and with a return to his normal accent. 'There could be repercussions if one put a load of shot up the wrong arse.'

'The Law's no help?'

'The Law? Does the Law repay you for your shepherding, for the work you've put into training your dogs, and the lambing, and building up your flock? Are you covered even

13

for market value? I don't know about the Law.' The face turned away and the voice seemed to come through fur. '*We've* allus been the Law,' Rumney said.

Harper cocked his head. 'Someone's singing.'

'It'll be Arabella; well, there's enough milk for the two of you. You don't want it cooled tonight, do you? I'll finish Isbell and you can take what I've got here.'

A figure came and stood in the doorway, cheeks and eyes shining, breath steaming in the lamplight.

'Who's that?' The girl peered at Harper, her accent charmingly American. 'A glow-worm would give a better light than this, Uncle Zeke.'

'Wrong season for glow-worms. It's George Harper.'

'Oh, good evening, Mr Harper. Isn't it a lovely night? Are we all waiting for milk?'

'Isbell's holding back,' Rumney complained. 'She's a cow that likes all the attention. You could do something for me, Harper, while you're waiting.'

'What's that?'

'There's a pile of eggs in the end manger; Arabella will give them to you. I promised them to Lucy Fell: guinea fowl eggs. If you take them to Thornbarrow you could earn a sherry for your pains.'

'I find Mrs Fell a little domineering,' Harper said doubtfully.

'You don't have to be afraid of her,' Arabella told him. 'She's interested only in rich gentlemen. She went after Uncle Zeke when they first came here but soon dropped him when she realised all his assets were in land and stock. Those gorgeous rings are far more portable than cows.'

'She was a married woman when she came here!' Rumney protested.

'I'm not saying she's promiscuous,' she said earnestly, 'but she's a lady who'd always have an insurance policy, isn't she? And Mr Fell wasn't a fit man, you could see that.'

'How do you know? You weren't here. He died three years back.'

14

'Grannie told me.'

'Your grandmother gossips. At eighty-five—'

'Gossip's not amusement, Uncle Zeke.' Arabella was grave. 'It's an essential part of social life.'

'Why?'

'It keeps up the moral values of a community by picking out the deviants and criticising their behaviour.'

'Are you suggesting Lucy Fell's a deviant?'

'No—o.' She considered this carefully. 'Perhaps not; the healthy, intelligent courtesan has always been respected. The Victorians said she took the pressure off respectable ladies. There's a number of unattached men in this dale,' she added darkly.

There was a pause. 'She frightens me,' Harper admitted eventually. 'I hide below the window-sill when I see her coming. She's been across to my place, you know.'

'She always takes something,' Arabella assured him. 'A pie or a jar of preserve: that's a courtship display. Are you a misogynist, Mr Harper?'

'I'm not sure—'

'Arabella!' Rumney broke in. 'We've no idea what you're on about! And suppose Lucy Fell came up for extra milk?'

'And heard us talking? Uncle Zeke, if you think Lucy doesn't know her own limitations by this time, you've learned nothing from the relationship.'

'I haven't had a relationship with her.'

'Everyone relates. We're all relating in this cow-shed. You relate to Isbell.'

'Couldn't you take the eggs to Thornbarrow,' he pleaded, 'and come back and tell us what Lucy Fell says about relating?'

'I'll do that some day but right now I have to make a caper sauce for the mutton so I must take the milk back, and if you don't hurry with that cow, Uncle Zeke, the mutton will go dry waiting for you.'

15

'There are two more cows yet, and the eggs to go to Thornbarrow.'

'Mr Harper will take the eggs on his way home.'

Rumney filled their cans with the warm milk. Something insubstantial as a shadow slid over Harper's feet and he jumped.

'Drat that pawky cat,' Rumney muttered. 'Always stands underneath when I'm pouring milk.'

Thornbarrow and Sandale House, where the Rumneys lived, and their buildings, formed a kind of street. Harper, a small bucket of eggs cradled in his arms, dangling the milk-can from three fingers, stepped gingerly down the cobbles towards the bridge and round the back of Thornbarrow, having difficulty with the gate. After the darkness between the barns, Lucy Fell's kitchen light made her garden look naked: the rocks shining with frost crystals and her great yews too black to be real. He glanced upstream at his herd of elephants. They were still there.

His boots made no sound on the flagged path. He knocked on the back door and someone shouted to him to come in. He found and depressed the thumb latch and entered a stone passage. On his right was a dim room with the doorway to the kitchen in the opposite wall. He could see the end of a table and a stove.

'Who is it?'

'Harper. I've brought your eggs from Zeke.'

He glanced round the living room. The oak table was set for dinner with glass and silver, and two red candles stood in pewter sticks. Only one standard lamp was lit. Firelight flickered on cream walls and on a magnificent bread cupboard at least six feet long and stretching from floor to ceiling. The date on it was 1649 and it formed the partition between the room and the kitchen.

'I can't come,' she called, still not showing herself. 'I'm piping.'

'What's that?'

'Come here, man, and stop shouting.'

He removed his boots in the passage and crossed the carpet: a spare but unremarkable middle-aged man with restless eyes. Lucy Fell looked up from the kitchen table and smiled. She wore a flame-coloured velvet gown with a butcher's apron protecting it and her tawny hair was looped in soft wings to a pleat at the back of her head.

'You're a lovely man,' she said when she saw the eggs, 'to come all this way on a bitter night for a poor widow woman.'

'I've only come from Zeke's cow-house. It was on my way actually.'

Her mouth drooped. 'You need a drink.'

She had been piping cream round a flan. The big wooden table was cluttered with the equipment and discarded trimmings of a luxurious meal. The smells—of rich gravy, spices, some kind of roasting bird—were delicious. She put the flan in the refrigerator, washed her hands and went to the bread cupboard where the drinks were. He accepted a whisky.

'How much would it be worth?' he asked, looking at the cupboard.

'You like it, don't you? I saw you were interested when you came to my party. I don't know what it would fetch. I'm not selling.'

'Just a thought.'

He noticed that she wasn't drinking. There was a bottle of red wine on the table, and champagne glasses. His eyes were expressionless. Places were laid only for two people.

'You must come and have a meal one night,' she remarked, watching him. 'Only a few friends, not a big party.'

'Mm. I'll do that.' She waited. 'I like this place,' he went on heavily. 'Tonight it's very remote: us all on our own up here, just a handful of houses. Very grim, some people would think: bleak.' He gestured towards the table. 'I like this; it's homely.'

Her fine eyebrows had risen. 'I don't know why you ever left London if you feel like that.'

He looked away. 'It gets a bit too much sometimes.'

'The rat race?' she asked ironically.

He nodded. 'Everything: noise, hurry, fumes; you never know where you are. You don't stay long in London yourself when you go there, do you?'

'That's different; my home's here, but London's so exciting! Sandale must seem incredibly dull to you. Besides, there's your work. . . . But I forgot: you're retired; you made tools of some kind. . .? What do you find to do over at Burblethwaite in these long evenings?'

'Most nights I fall asleep in front of the television. Business had been difficult for me for some time and after all the worry of the past year I don't feel up to much. I'm glad of the rest— which is why I came here, of course. I seem to spend more and more time in bed as I get older.' He smiled ruefully. 'I'm nearly a pensioner, you know. What do you do in the evenings?'

'There's the Women's Institute, the Red Cross, lectures in Carnthorpe and Carlisle; other people's parties, planning the garden for next year, cooking for the freezer; it can take a whole evening to make one course if you're interested in that kind of thing. There are books and television and listening to music. My life is quite full.'

'We're both self-sufficient then. I suppose people would have to be, in a place like this; they've always had to make their own amusements.'

She smiled a trifle stiffly and the telephone started to ring. It stood on a table by a curtained window and she crossed the room with long strides, her skirt swaying and catching the firelight.

'Yes?' she asked pleasantly, not giving her number, looking

18

past her visitor to the fire. Harper stared at his whisky intently.

'No, he isn't—' Her tone was suddenly harsh and she turned her back, gripping the edge of the table so hard that the knuckles gleamed white. A voice shrilled at the other end of the line then stopped as if the speaker had choked. 'I'll give him your message,' Lucy said with elaborate contempt. 'He may call you back.'

She put the receiver down carefully and shivered, but the room was warm. Taking a marquetry box from the cupboard, she came back to the fire and offered him a cigarette. In silence he lit hers, then his own. It tasted stale. Her hands were steady but she watched him through the smoke and her eyes held speculation.

'Zeke tells me he's missing some sheep,' he said.

'Oh yes?'

'He thinks someone rustled them—is that the word?'

'Surely you rustle cattle; you steal sheep. People used to be hanged for sheep stealing, I believe.'

'Zeke said something about shooting the chap if he could catch him.'

'The Rumneys are a law unto themselves. When Zeke says they've lived here for five hundred years you get the feeling he means it personally. He doesn't distinguish between his ancestors and the present generations. Grannie Rumney's the same; they're all damned autocratic.'

'Arabella's an odd girl; I can't get her measure at all.'

She shot a glance at him. 'She's a real Rumney; Grannie says that's why Dolly Banks—that's Arabella's mother—why her husbands keep running away: even Americans can't take a Rumney bossing them about.' She pursed her lips. 'Dolly Banks has got an eye for the main chance though: rich husbands and enormous alimonies and no hard feelings. Grannie says Arabella will come into a fortune when she's twenty-one.'

'It's nice to have money.' He was wistful.

19

'Another drink? No? Well, it's nice to be able to offer guests a drink; imagine, if you could only afford beer and instant coffee! And fancy making shin beef and potatoes the focal point of a dinner.' She glanced at her table complacently. 'I don't want to be rich like Dolly and Arabella but I'd find poverty rather tiresome. Subsistence level is good enough for me providing I've got the basic necessities.' She smiled. 'I don't have to sell the bread cupboard yet.'

Harper's eyes rested on her rings and he blinked slowly. 'I understand Arabella is going to start a pony trekking business in the dale.'

She gave a snort of derision. 'That's Jackson Wren's idea.'

'Wren's behind it, is he?'

'Well, it's obvious. Jackson, who is *not* one of the world's workers, as you must have noticed, would like to start trekking but he hasn't any money. Arabella is an expert on horses, has access to a lot of money, and is fascinated by Jackson. It seems a shaky foundation for business but I doubt if it will ever get off the ground because one of the Rumneys, Zeke or Grannie or even Dolly, will put their foot down as soon as Arabella tries to transfer money from the States. What's your interest in the Rumneys anyway?'

'In Arabella,' he corrected. 'She's so—foreign—for Sandale, and then I'd seen her with Wren and wondered. . . . And then tonight she came for the milk while I was talking to Zeke, and she seemed such a well-educated girl. Wren's not up to much, is he? Father a Council worker?'

She was amused. 'You're a snob. At a guess I'd say the relationship is the usual one between a girl and a virile man.' She was perched on the arm of an easy chair and now she regarded him with a lack of expression that possessed its own significance. 'Some of us still make our own amusements,' she murmured. 'Now how about that other half?' She rose and took his glass. Their fingers touched.

He got up quickly. 'I must go; I left my stew on the gas,

20

and you're expecting company. I just brought the eggs. . . .'

He was retreating towards the passage as he spoke. He thrust his feet into his gum boots, picked up his milk-can and fumbled for the latch. 'See you,' he threw back over his shoulder, testing the slates of the path for rime. Lucy's expression was strained.

Chapter 3

NOBLE WAS LATE, and in a bad mood. His face softened a little at the sight of Lucy's table but obviously he wasn't happy. He'd been drinking, too, which was unusual. On Friday nights he had been accustomed to come straight from the factory to Thornbarrow, not even calling at his own home at the mouth of the dale. True, there had been a disruption in this routine over the past few weeks but he might have been expected to return to the old arrangement without diversions. He knew this.

'I called and had a drink with Sarah,' he explained. He had to justify the drink anyway; she would smell the whisky on his breath.

'How is she?'

'Oh, you know Sarah: she can't take much in by six o'clock in the evening.' Lucy measured sherry carefully into a pan on the stove. He watched moodily, nursing a large Scotch. 'I wanted to see her before the weekend,' he went on. 'Things aren't going at all well.'

'At the factory?'

He nodded gloomily. 'I don't think we can keep it up; the bottom's dropped out of the market. For Christ's sake, people are economising on their own food!' He produced a superior kind of pet food. 'I thought if we introduced more cereals and used less meat, have a publicity campaign stressing how much healthier a cereal-based diet is—'

'Is it?'

'I don't know but I daresay we can find a boffin who will say so. But we need more capital: for new plant and for publicity, so I had to talk to Sarah. . . .' He stopped.

'And she wasn't amenable?'

22

'She suggested we sell the factory and start farming.'

'Oh, Denny!'

'Well, my sweet, at six o'clock! She's probably sunk half a bottle since this morning. She said, "I haven't a penny to spare, love, and with things the way they are, we ought to get out while the going's good and put the money into something that pays—like sheep." ' Lucy licked her lips. 'Don't look like that,' Noble admonished. 'She didn't mean it; I'll have another go at her Sunday morning—I'll take her up to Storms for a drink. Oh, you think that would be indiscreet? I suppose you're right. But I'll persuade her to let me have some money, you'll see. It's just that any request for cash she sees as a threat to her way of life: less money, less drink. She sees threats everywhere; hallucinogenic, that's the word.'

'Threats?'

'She's getting hallucinations. I'm terrified she'll have an accident—she must do sooner or later, but she won't give up driving. She's terrified herself. She said the old Escort had a lot of play in the steering, but the steering was as firm as a rock. But she bought this Marina and it's much more difficult for her to drive; she says she can't judge its width. Thank God she doesn't go out except in the mornings when she's relatively sober. D'you know what she asked me tonight?'

'No. What?'

'Would I stand by her if she killed someone.'

'What on earth was in her mind?'

'I don't know. Does the brain soften in these cases?'

'You'd have to ask a doctor. But one thing you should be thankful for: you haven't got a quarrelsome wife.'

'Ah, that *is* something. Poor Sarah; I don't think she's ever said a harsh word to me about you.'

Lucy looked astonished. 'Of course she wouldn't; she's grateful to me.'

'*Grateful?*'

'Darling, Sarah's terribly middle-class—so are you, of course—but in Sarah's book you just don't neglect husbands.

In sickness and in health, you know: all that bit. Sarah knows she can't make a decent home for you now, but I save her from being guilty. I take her place. Well? Don't I?'

'You do far more than that, my sweet.'

She smiled, pushed a pan to one side of the stove, and took a bottle of Veuve Clicquot from the refrigerator.

'We won't need ice for this,' she said, 'we'll drink it too quickly.'

In the living room they toasted each other and he sat and regarded the fire absently.

'George Harper called,' she told him. 'Zeke sent him down with the eggs. What an ordinary little man he is, and no topic of conversation at all. No manners; I don't mean he's rude exactly—it's that he has no idea of how to behave. He gawked at my dress and at the table, but obviously thought it wasn't done to compliment me or even to comment on the fact that I was entertaining. I gave him a whisky and he was as nervous as a cat but didn't know how to take his leave. I had to throw him out in the end.'

'How did you do that?'

'Very simple. One fits the means to the man. I propositioned him.'

'You didn't!'

'Don't worry; he's sitting in Burblethwaite now, burping over his stew and watching telly and wondering if he imagined it. Oh, I'm sure he'll be thinking that sex lies in the remote past for people of his age, so what on earth—? He'll think he's starting to have hallucinations. Surrey, he comes from, doesn't he? I see him in a semi with a pocket handkerchief garden and a rotary lawn mower—'

'No.'

'What d'you mean: no?'

'He's not suburban. He says he's a wholesale tool merchant. I should leave it at that.'

'Why, darling, you're not jealous of George Harper?'

He shook his head seriously. He looked very tired and the

fatigue was in his voice. 'No, I'm not worried about Harper. What's that delicious smell?"

Lucy changed gear smoothly. 'Which one? We're having kidneys in sherry for starters, a *carbonade* to follow, and grouse. There's a bilberry flan if you can manage it.'

'Now that's unfair: all my favourites in one night.'

By the time they reached the grouse, he was rather drunk and his beefy face was a dangerous red. Lucy said casually as she served him, 'That fire's too hot on your back; move round to the side and take off your jacket.'

He obeyed, scraping his chair. 'Had a bit too much to drink,' he said apologetically.

'The food will act as blotting paper, and you're not driving.'

'Blotting paper!' He regarded his grouse with reverence and giggled. 'One thing, you'll never be one of the millions of unemployed; you could get a position any day as a chef.' He returned to his plate. 'Perfect,' he said. 'Quite perfect.'

'Have some watercress; it's good for the blood.'

'You do take care of me, Lucy.'

She shrugged and helped herself to salad. She had no grouse. She leaned one elbow on the table and her arm, in the red velvet, made a pretty line in the soft light. Noble's eyes were held by her colour and sparkle but his concentration was on the food. They ate in a companionable silence for a while before she asked: 'Has Miles Mossop been in court yet?'

'Yes; while we were in town. I saw Hendry at lunch-time: the C.I.D. inspector. The magistrates refused to give Mossop the benefit of the doubt. I'm not surprised; he wouldn't make a good impression on the court. He's an uncouth bugger.' Lucy said nothing. Noble chewed stolidly, staring at a candle flame. At length he said, 'Curious about that crate of Scotch; a chap in his position doesn't have to buy the odd crate that fell off the back of a lorry, but it was stolen all right, and just the one.'

'Could someone have planted it in his cellar?'

'Would they? I doubt it: too expensive a gesture. But he's a fellow without principles; perhaps someone had it outside in the boot of a car and offered it to him at a discount. He'd know it was stolen, of course. Point is: who else knew? Someone was after Mossop's blood. Hendry told me: the police got a tip-off about that whisky.'

'Who from?'

'Anonymous. You'd expect it to be a waiter or someone else who'd left under a cloud, but he hasn't sacked anyone for six months.'

'It's someone who's still there then, who hates him quietly. That must be an unpleasant thought for him.'

'There's no staff at Storms during the winter. It's the person who tipped off the police who'll be having a bad time now: wondering if Mossop suspects him, and what he'll do if he finds out.'

The latch of the back door clicked. She glanced up quickly but Noble, crumbling a roll, had heard nothing. The inner door was flung open and a girl stood there, a girl with short yellow hair and a vapid little face which was now sharp and ugly. She wore a huge bottle-green coat and her head was sunk between her shoulders as if she had no neck. Her eyes were quite mad.

Lucy's face was blank. Noble looked up, followed her glance and froze. The girl's face didn't change. She stared at him with unbearable intensity. Her hands were hidden in her wide sleeves and she shivered spasmodically.

'Why didn't you call back?' Her voice rose, almost out of control.

Noble was speechless and it was Lucy who responded. 'Come in and shut the door; both doors.'

Noble turned to her and said, with the elaborate diction of

26

a drunk fighting to get a grip on himself: 'What would you like me to do?'

Lucy said with the faintest smile, 'If Peta won't, perhaps you would close the doors.'

He got up carefully, holding the edge of the table and testing his legs.

Peta Mossop repeated tonelessly, 'Why didn't you ring me?'

'I didn't tell him,' Lucy said, and took a sip of her claret. 'Won't you sit down?'

Noble had stopped in the centre of the room. 'What didn't you tell me?'

'It's bitterly cold with both doors open,' Lucy reminded him tightly.

He jerked into action, blundered past the girl and slammed the outer door. Lucy's chin rose a fraction. He closed the living room door with exaggerated care. Peta made no move to sit down. He glanced at Lucy and drew out the chair that had its back to the fire.

'Won't you take your coat off?' he asked, then frowned at himself. Peta sat down, still staring at him.

'I rang earlier. She said she'd tell you. I should have known she wouldn't.'

Noble asked helplessly of Lucy, 'What ought we to do?'

She stood up, collecting the plates. 'I'll make some coffee.'

He picked up a dish and followed her out to the kitchen. 'What shall we do?' he whispered urgently. 'Is she drunk? What did she ring about?'

'She was hysterical—like she is now. A brandy might calm her down, then I'll get rid of her. She's out to make trouble.'

'Shall I ring Miles to come and fetch her?'

'I don't think that would be a good idea, darling.'

She looked up. The girl stood in the doorway, and now there was feeling in her eyes. She regarded Lucy malevolently.

'I know you're talking about me—'

27

'We could hardly talk in front of you,' Lucy said reasonably. She advanced on the other with the coffee tray. 'You'll stay and have coffee with us before you go?'

Peta stood aside and followed her back to the table. Lucy took a bottle of brandy from the cupboard and poured a generous measure for the girl.

'Sit down; you look cold. Did you walk here?'

'Yes.'

Peta tasted the brandy and then drank half of it. Noble gave her a cigarette. He lit it and she leaned back, sighing and exhaling smoke. Her eyes were calmer, too calm.

'I shouldn't have come.' No one responded to that. 'Although,' she went on thoughtfully, 'brandy and a smoke couldn't make me relax in the flat; I know: I tried it. I flipped. It's all right now, at this moment, even with you there—' She looked across the table at Lucy whose expression was coolly attentive as she poured coffee. Noble sat down carefully, halfway between the two women. 'But when I get back to the flat,' Peta went on, 'and start waiting for the telephone to ring, I can't stand it—and I shan't sleep even with the pills. . . .' She looked round the room. 'You don't know what it's like,' she told Noble. 'You've got it made; you're all so sure of yourselves, even your wife.'

'My wife!'

Her lip curled. 'Oh, we've spoken—occasionally. She doesn't care about anything, does she? An alcoholic, money to burn, and hard as nails. What's she got to lose? Why should she be afraid of me?'

'Why should anyone?' Lucy asked.

The girl looked at her with hatred. 'Someone sent me a letter.'

'Oh.' Noble stiffened and turned to Lucy. 'D'you think—?' She shook her head at him. 'What did it say?' he asked, turning back.

A shutter came down over Peta's eyes and she drank the rest of her brandy. 'It's not just the letter,' she said, not answering the question. 'There are telephone calls.' She looked at him deliberately. 'The caller never says anything, just holds the phone and after a while he puts it down.' She shuddered.

'There were telephone calls before,' Noble said sternly, 'weren't there?'

'Not really.' She was apathetic. 'I imagined them.' Her head sank into her shoulders again, like a rabbit waiting for the stoat.

'Has anything ever been said on the telephone?'

'No.'

'Nothing happens?'

'Just breathing.' She sighed loudly. 'No, maybe I made that up, about the breathing. I can't be sure. Silence,' she went on. 'He never speaks. It's driving me crazy.' She put her elbows on the table and her face in her hands. Noble and Lucy exchanged glances. He indicated the brandy and she shrugged. He half-filled the girl's glass, spilling some.

'And these anonymous letters?' he pressed, 'what did they say?'

Peta raised her head and stared at him, then looked meaningly at the other woman.

'Have you brought them with you?' Noble asked.

'I only had one. I lost it.'

'You lost it.' His tone was heavy with irony.

'I put it in my handbag and it disappeared.'

He opened his mouth to expostulate but thought better of it. 'Have you told Miles?'

'You're mad!'

Suddenly he had a revelation. 'Have you told *Quentin*?'

She had been pale when she entered, had recovered some colour sitting close to the fire, but now the blood drained out of her face and her eyes were stark with something like fear.

'But I think he's just the person,' Noble protested. 'He's your doctor, and a good one; he knows your history—I mean, we all have a history, don't we? How about going to Quentin first thing tomorrow, eh?' The tone was avuncular.

There was a long silence during which Peta looked round the room and avoided Lucy's gaze. Once or twice she opened her mouth as if to say something but didn't.

'You have to think of yourself,' Lucy told her.

The girl stood up and said spitefully, 'I'm sorry I intruded. Don't get up; I'll let myself out.'

Noble was still struggling to his feet as she opened the door. When they heard the latch click into place he turned to Lucy in horror. 'She's round the bend!' She nodded unhappily. 'What's she after? Attention, sympathy?'

'Or you?' But she wasn't joking; she was preoccupied.

'Could be,' he agreed without selfconsciousness, and shivered. 'Quentin will deal with her. After all, he had her before—treated her, I mean, when she had that first break-down. He'll send her back to the same specialist. Wonder why she's gone like this again? You know, if she's made it all up —I mean, we know the phone calls are imaginary, so the anonymous letter—? There was the one you had.... It looks as if she's writing them, doesn't it? You don't lose anonymous letters; you keep them or you burn them, but they're far too valuable—or incriminating—to lose.' He sighed and shook his head. 'Such a pretty girl too; how she's spoilt herself. I blame Mossop for a lot of it. She hasn't a penny to spend on herself; has to go to him on her knees for the price of a pair of tights.'

Lucy said coldly, 'Well, if she goes on her knees.... But that slit-sided number she had on at my party, the night she did the Mata Hari act with you, cost all of fifty quid, even made in Hong Kong.'

'Oh yes, she told me it cost a bomb, but he paid for it. He likes to see her well dressed, says it's an advertisement for the place.' Lucy stood up and started to stack the coffee tray. 'Of course, they should have had children,' he went on.

'Makes all the difference.' He beamed vacuously at his brandy. 'I'll have a word with Quentin tomorrow. He should know about this because she may not go to him unless she's pushed, and I feel a certain respons...' He checked and threw a startled glance towards the kitchen, then got to his feet heavily. 'It's a pity,' he said, 'a great pity.'

Chapter 4

'I HAD A rough night,' Jackson Wren told Rumney, 'I couldn't eat me breakfast.'

'You can eat it when we get back,' Rumney said sourly. 'We're late starting as it is.'

They were taking some sheep down to winter on the doctor's meadows. At this hour of the morning there was no sun in the bottom and the fields were white with frost. The sky held a pallid glare but it was hardly bright enough to warrant Jackson Wren's dark glasses. He was a large brawny fellow with fair hair cut short, a deep tan and a scrubby moustache. He could have been a warrant officer from a good foot regiment. He was dressed in breeches, navy socks with white snowflakes, lightweight boots and an immense scarlet padded jacket. He walked with a lurch, his hands in his pockets and his head low.

Beside him Zeke Rumney had the same hunched stoop though his came not from any studied imitation of hard men but from carelessness. All Arabella's insistence on good posture passed over her uncle's head. Seen in the daylight Rumney was a powerful man in his sixties, more than six feet tall, taller than Wren who was half his age. Wisps of grey hair stuck out from under his battered cap but his eyebrows were dark and heavy, the eyes a blue from which most of the colour had gone. Despite the bitterness of this November morning he wore an ancient jersey under bib-and-brace overalls, and a decrepit jacket with the elbows gone, of a shade between earth and dung. It had no buttons and it had been made for him when he was up at Oxford. Now he eyed the other's duvet jacket thoughtfully.

Wren was immediately aware of the interest. 'Same as they

wear on Everest,' he said casually, extending an arm. 'Thirty-five quid.'

'It looks like it. You could have bought a pony for that.'

'I've got no cold-weather gear. For rescues, I mean.'

Rumney turned back to his sheep: hoggs, and young gimmers which wouldn't be breeding this year. He thought that the animals had gone back a bit; there was no grass left for them on the tops—but they'd pick up on Quentin Bright's meadows.

He was accompanied by four dogs: three Border collies and a brindled lurcher. The oldest collie had a grizzled muzzle and a limp but its face was brilliant with concentration. The other two were siblings: young and so eager that they had to keep circling tightly to avoid over-running the sheep.

'I don't know why you needed me,' Wren remarked with forced joviality. 'You could have had t'dogs going ahead to warn traffic.'

'The post comes early,' Rumney reminded him. 'I'm not having my best dogs killed by yon daft driver belting round Storms' bend—and hitting a few of our fat lambs into t'bargain.'

'Fat lambs! Reckon them what's missing got blown away if these is anything to go by.'

Rumney turned cold eyes on him. 'Who told you Ah were missing sheep?'

Wren slashed at a bramble with his stick and the lurcher jumped backwards. 'Someone,' he said airily, the dark glasses giving nothing away. 'You're missing some, aren't you?'

Rumney's jaw set hard but he said nothing further at that moment. Ahead of the flock the bottom of a drive showed on the right of the lane, with a track climbing the hill among mature and well-spaced trees.

He sent the old dog forward. The sheep blocked the way and the collie jumped up and ran lightly over their backs. The animals trotted on unconcerned, bearing leftwards a little, giving the gateway a respectable berth where the dog stood with straddled forelegs and a fierce grin.

'Time you got in front,' Rumney said. 'Post van tears round this bend like a hell's—'

'He's got to slow down to turn in Storms' drive.'

'What's up then?' Rumney was staring ahead.

The foremost sheep which, after the entrance to the drive, had spread back to fill the lane, were shouldering leftwards again, then trying to turn back.

'There's no car coming,' Wren protested.

The rear half of the flock, pushed by dogs and men, crowded the front ranks and these, unable to force a way back, were burrowing and pushing sideways so that the pattern, fluid as water, became concave, then broke as they raced away up the left side of the lane, brushing the hedge and leaping high in the air as they passed one point.

'Sod it,' Wren exclaimed, uncomprehending.

'There must be something in the ditch over there,' Rumney said, advancing. 'There is; it's an old coat.'

Three of the dogs watched his face to see what they were meant to do about the sheep but the fourth, receiving no orders, darted to the ditch and the dark green coat (which the men saw now was not old at all), and they heard his claws scrabble as he braked. Then his head and tail went down and he yelped and ran: back up the lane towards Sandale House.

Rumney flicked a finger at the remaining dogs and they tore down the lane to turn the sheep. He stooped to the coat but where his original intention had been to pick it up, it was now obvious that he couldn't. There was someone inside it, fitting the ditch too well, one trousered leg visible from the knee to the foot in a red suède shoe and the leg in too strained a position for the owner to be asleep. The coat hid the head but they realised that what had looked like a swathe of bright straw was hair.

'She's been hit by a car,' Wren was saying. He sounded terrified. 'I saw her last night: up t'lane a ways; her was weaving all over t'road. That's t'second in this spot. Is she all right?'

The sheep pattered back to halt in a heaving barrier across the lane.

'Watch they don't get by,' Rumney muttered.

He knelt on one knee and gently eased down the needle-cord collar. Behind him Wren gasped. The profile was unmarked, the lips parted and the eyes wide but the hair on top of the skull was matted with blood. Rumney covered the head again and got to his feet. Wren was on his knees on the grass verge.

'We've got to get these gimmers off t'road,' Rumney said. 'Look sharp, Jackson, and go an' open t'gate.'

The other shook his head dumbly, still bowed over the grass retching. Rumney's lips set, he looked beyond the sheep to his dogs and called back the old collie. Dog and man changed places neatly and the farmer lumbered ahead of the flock round the almost right-angled corner they called Storms' bend. A hundred yards ahead there was a gate into the meadows on the left. Beyond the gate the road was clear and he slowed to a walk.

The dogs held the sheep between them while he opened the gate, then the flock streamed through and Wren appeared round the bend his lurch less obvious, his face grey.

'I should have had me breakfast,' he complained.

'Go and get t'doctor. I'll stay down here.'

'What'll I tell 'im?'

'Just tell him there's a body in t'ditch.'

'But it's Peta Mossop!'

'Give over waffling, lad, and get cracking; we haven't got all day.'

Wren swallowed and started down the lane, passing the foot of the drive leading to High Hollins where the Nobles lived. Rumney and the dogs went back round Storms' bend.

He wouldn't have long to wait; the doctor's house was less than a quarter of a mile past Noble's. It was possible that, being a Saturday morning, Quentin wouldn't be at home, but then he remembered how early they were in bringing the sheep down and he pulled a half-hunter from an inside pocket. It was just on nine o'clock.

The dogs hung back, and out of regard for them he stopped before he came to the body. The sun had not yet reached this side of the valley although the brackeny slopes opposite were brilliant in the light. It was bitterly cold. He looked across the water-meadows between him and the gorge they called the Throat and tried to give his attention to sheep, and the wisdom of putting animals down here at the back-end. Reflecting on the possibility of flooding was a constructive activity. Waiting by a dead body served no purpose. If it had been a sheep now, he'd have gone home for a spade, or taken an organ for the vet to analyse, or sent for the vet.

He heard a car changing up fast behind him and, recognising the sound of the doctor's engine, he started walking again, calling the dogs to heel. Bright's Maxi overtook him on the bend with two people up, and stopped. As the doctor got out, Rumney called, 'Let Jackson take the car on or you'll cause another accident, parking here.'

Bright turned and spoke to Wren who moved over to the driver's seat and drove on.

'Well,' the doctor said by way of greeting. 'What the hell!'

He stooped to the body and lifted the coat collar. At sight of the wound he drew in his breath with an audible hiss. He touched the skin of the forehead and, putting a hand on the jaw, turned it easily towards him. An arc of false eyelashes detached itself from an eyelid and dropped in the ditch. The left cheek was reddened as if bruised, but not extensively.

'A car, d'you think?' Rumney asked in a neutral tone.

'What else?' The tone was bitter and defeated. 'They come round this bend like bats out of hell. It's not three months since the last one. The Council will have to take that corner off now—and two people have to be killed before they'll make a move.'

'Plenty of drivers have managed to get round here without killing anyone.'

'But two people in three months!'

Rumney nodded. 'And they never caught the other one, but that was in summer time.' He looked down. 'It's no good speculating on who did this: a local, or someone who'd had too much up at Storms, or a visitor. . . . Tourists in November? I wonder what she was doing down on the road. You'll have to get on to the police.'

'And there's Mossop to be told.'

'I'll come with you; it's better for two of us to be there when he's told, just in case . . .'

Bright covered the ghastly head and they started to walk up the lane. The dogs, who had been sitting a few yards towards Sandale in a patch of sun, got to their feet with alacrity and trotted with them.

Quentin Bright strode jerkily and fast, not waiting for the other. He was a thin man with receding hair and passionate eyes. He worked like a horse, involved himself too much with his patients, was often ill to the point of physical debility but was saved from ultimate collapse by his nice dull managing wife. Arriving now at his car, he stared at Jackson Wren as though wondering what to do with him.

It was Rumney who gave the orders. 'Go back and wait there till the police come, and make sure no one interferes with it.'

'Why the police?' Wren asked anxiously, getting out of the car.

In the act of easing into the passenger seat Rumney raised his big head and bared his teeth. 'What time did tha see her in t'road?'

'Late on; she were straying all over t'lane. I nearly—' He stopped and the open mouth and opaque lenses were three black holes in his face.

Rumney shrugged. 'The police will sort it out.'

37

'*When* did he see her?' Bright asked as they drove up the Storms track.

'Last night.'

'Do you think he hit her? Was he drunk?'

'He'd been drinking but if he'd hit her he wouldn't have told me he'd seen her; he's not that much of a fool. When you consider, he's not normally nearly so silly as he's behaving now; it's shock—and that's in his favour. No, he didn't hit her—I wouldn't think.'

'Someone did.' Bright halted the car on the sweep outside the Storms hotel. They stared through the windscreen at the mountains which looked very clear and close.

'Foul play?' Rumney asked.

'Well, she didn't do that to herself,' Bright said acidly. 'Here's Mossop.'

They got out of the car slowly and deliberately. Miles Mossop was a fat man who had once been powerful; he had the body of a wrestler gone to seed. He was dressed in wrinkled jeans and a grubby shirt strained over his obese stomach. He had long thin ginger hair with a bald patch, luxuriant sideburns and pale grey eyes. His face was large, soft and sagging, and he regarded them with an expression of irony tinged with contempt. If he was surprised by the appearance of the doctor he didn't show it although his eyes did rest for a puzzled moment on Rumney in his working clothes. They greeted him and he grunted a response. The doctor looked past him to the hall.

'What's up?' Mossop asked.

'We've got bad news for you.'

The publican's face was blank. 'About what?'

'Peta.'

'What's happened to her?' The eyes flickered to Rumney.

'She's been hit by a car.'

'Where?'

'Just near the foot of the drive.' Bright's voice climbed as if the position of the body had suddenly astonished him.

'I haven't been in her room,' Mossop said. He sounded dazed. Bright started to speak but the other went on flatly, as if he guessed the answer. 'How bad is she?'

There was a pause in which Rumney threw a glance at the doctor, obviously wondering whether he should give more than moral support, a pause during which Mossop's face lost its hostility and his jaw dropped, and the doctor, relieved that the other had guessed the truth, nodded.

'She'd been dead for a long time, Miles.... She died immediately.'

The man's mouth snapped shut and he glared at them, his head swinging from one to the other like a bull threatened on two fronts, then he turned his back and went into the hotel. The others exchanged a glance and followed.

He'd gone to the cocktail bar where he drew himself a large whisky and drained it at a gulp. He made a move to pour another then checked and, turning, put both hands on the counter, still holding the empty glass, and glared at them.

'I can't take it in. Dead. You did say she's dead?'

'There's no doubt, Miles.'

His look was stricken. 'What do I do?' he whispered.

'You can't do anything at the moment,' Bright pointed out, 'I'll have to report it to the police—'

'Will they be bringing her here? The wife?'

Bright looked at Rumney. Suddenly Mossop cried: 'How does *he* come into it? Did he find her?'

'I was putting the gimmers in the meadows,' Rumney explained easily, 'Jackson Wren was with me.'

'When did it happen?'

Bright said, 'I haven't—it's impossible to say, yet.'

Rumney said, 'There was hardly any frost on the coat—' and stopped.

Mossop's eyes opened wide. 'She were out last night.'

'Where?'

'I don't know. I saw her go out about nine, nine-thirty. I

didn't see her come back. You haven't told me what happened down there.'

'She had head injuries,' Bright said.

'Is that what did it?'

'I haven't done a full examination but—it would be the head injury, yes.'

'Was she on t'road?'

'In the ditch, as if she'd—'

'As if what?'

'As if the car had thrown her there.'

Bright turned away and caught Rumney's eye. The doctor had been about to say 'as if she'd been put there'. He was used to seeing death from violence, impact deaths, and he was thinking that, for a body that had been thrown in the ditch by a car, it looked terribly neat.

Chapter 5

P ETA M OSSOP'S BODY was found on Saturday and the resulting revelations shocked the dale, but for reasons of age or personal problems some people were able, as the week wore on, to forget about Peta, at least for short periods. At Sandale House on the following Friday afternoon, old Mrs Rumney and her granddaughter, Arabella, regarded the scones and cakes on the kitchen table and speculated on nothing more sinister than the present whereabouts of Zeke.

Grannie Rumney was pear-shaped with narrow shoulders and broad hips. Her hair was white and fine, drawn back to a plaited bun at the nape of her neck, and she had deep, hooded eyes: the eyes of a matriarchal turtle. At eighty-five her sight was not so good as it had been and, although she didn't bump into furniture and could still measure ingredients when she was cooking, she gave the impression of looking beyond the object of her regard. Arabella said she was a seer.

'When do we take it to the other room?' the girl asked, indicating the food. She wore a white jersey and a red flannel skirt to below her knees, and Lapp boots. With her curling black hair and the deep Rumney eyes—a very dark blue in her case—she was a vivid complement to the old lady.

'We don't set the table till she comes.' There was reproof in the tone. 'Food would look bad in the room, catching dust.'

'It's doing that here.'

'She can't see it though.'

'I wonder what she's really like,' Arabella mused, going to stand in the window. 'Tough as old boots, Zeke says; all leather brogues and Scottish tweeds: everybody's maiden aunt —that's what he said, and a climber and a lawyer as well. What a wild mixture!'

41

'No, it's your uncle's old friend, Ted Roberts, who's the retired lawyer. This lady is *his* friend; I believe there's an understanding between them.' Arabella stared. 'She writes love stories,' Grannie continued, 'and she's a magistrate and Mr Roberts says she'll catch the man who's stealing our sheep.'

'I don't believe it,' Arabella breathed. 'There's Zeke; oh look, he hasn't changed his clothes!'

Rumney and the old collie came in the back door (which was in the front of the house but called the back to distinguish it from the main entrance which was down the street a bit). He regarded his womenfolk and the food anxiously.

'I hope she's not going to be late,' he said. 'Penelope looks as if she's coming down.'

'*Coming down?*' Arabella glowed with delight.

'Calving—and she's one you have to be with all the time; she frets on her own.'

The dog pricked his ears and stared at the door. Rumney cocked his head. Grannie, who appeared to be counting the scones, asked, 'Is that her?' A dark Austin 1100 slid to a halt outside the window.

There was the familiar movement of a lady picking up her handbag from the passenger seat, then the driver's door opened and Miss Pink stood up smoothing her skirt and regarding the façade of Sandale House approvingly from behind thick spectacles. Rumney and the collie went out by the back door in order to admit her ceremoniously by way of the main entrance. Arabella and Grannie went through to the living room, carefully shutting the door behind them to keep animals out of the kitchen.

Everyone entered the living room by different doors and Grannie launched into a little speech of welcome while Arabella took stock of the visitor.

There were the brogues: beautifully polished with huge serrated tongues; ribbed brown stockings, and a coat and skirt in a tweed which fairly reeked of peat smoke. The shirt was in cream silk and the brooch at Miss Pink's throat was a cairngorm. Her hair was thick, grey and tapered by an expert, her face round and roughened by Cornish gales. The frames of her spectacles were large, in a fetching marbled green. She carried a tan leather handbag and soft brown gloves.

She greeted them, smiled at Grannie and Arabella and allowed herself to be seated in the best chair, which was placed by the range and opposite the jutting partition which protected the hearth from draughts. Having calculated how long she might withstand the heat from the fire, she had a momentary qualm when she observed that what she had taken for a very large dog on the hearth-rug was coloured curiously in the firelight and had far too many little legs, perfectly formed. When Arabella switched on a light this was revealed as a number of sleeping cats in an arrangement reminiscent of Hieronymus Bosch but more pleasing.

She answered polite questions about the journey from Cornwall and, after a decent interval, Grannie went out to the kitchen and Arabella started to bring in the food. As Miss Pink chatted she absorbed the atmosphere of this large low-ceilinged room where massive oak pieces stood in the shadows, hams hung from hooks, and twin seventeenth-century spice cupboards were set in the plastered wall either side of the Victorian range.

Tea arrived, with home-made scones. Rumney drank delicately, his cup held in large red hands, the fingers swollen from working in the cold. Arabella explained about her being American and that normally she lived in Texas and that her mother had just parted from her second husband so Arabella had come to England not because she was unhappy but to let the others work things out, as she put it. Then she stopped talking because she thought other people's marital affairs were boring. There was a break in the conversation.

Grannie asked politely: 'Do you think you'll like the Lakes?'

'I like them already,' Miss Pink pointed out. 'I've often

come here on holiday; I've even walked down Sandale, but I've never spent any length of time here.'

'I don't think you'll have to now,' Grannie said.

Rumney turned his head inquiringly to his mother and Miss Pink asked carefully, 'What makes you think that, Mrs Rumney?'

The old lady looked at a spot over the visitor's shoulder. 'You'll soon find who killed Peta Mossop,' she said.

There was a short silence and then Arabella said, 'I thought Miss Pink had come here to try to find out who was stealing our sheep?'

Rumney stirred. 'I'll have to go and look at Penelope in quarter of an hour.' Miss Pink's brows rose. 'My cow,' he explained. He looked at the old lady. 'Mother is very perceptive. . . .' Grannie watched the flames, her face expressionless. 'I've only spoken to Miss Pink on the phone,' he reminded his family, 'so she doesn't know what's been happening: not the latest developments.'

'You've found out who stole the sheep?' Miss Pink asked politely.

'Oh no. No. By the latest developments I meant the post mortem and the inquest on Peta Mossop. I told you that there'd been an accident at Storms' bend; you'll know the place if you know the dale. Well, it wasn't an accident.'

Silence.

'It was murder,' Arabella said.

Miss Pink frowned, unable for a moment to bridge the gap between stolen sheep and murder.

'The inquest was adjourned,' Rumney said. 'Her face was bruised and the post mortem found that the bruise was made some time before death—not long, but it didn't coincide with the blow on the skull that killed her. That was caused by some blunt instrument. And they think she was put in the ditch late at night, or rather, in the early hours of Saturday morning because there wasn't much frost on the coat, and the fields were white. She was definitely put there; she'd died somewhere

44

else and been moved—something to do with post mortem staining? And then the wound had bled the wrong way, you see, for how the body was lying in the ditch.'

Miss Pink followed this attentively but Grannie could have been listening to a report on the sheep sales.

'On Friday night,' Rumney went on, 'Peta was at Lucy Fell's place—that's the house opposite, down past our barn. Lucy's a widow and friendly with Denis Noble who was with her that night. Peta turned up after dinner, uninvited and rather drunk, and left about ten-thirty. They seem to have been the last people to see her alive. Mossop saw her go out about nine-thirty but didn't see her come back. The police grilled him for forty-eight hours—he says—but apparently they couldn't shake his story.'

'What's that?' Miss Pink asked. 'In detail?'

'He closed early: around ten-thirty, and then he says he checked that there were no cigarettes burning anywhere and went to bed. Peta wasn't around but he didn't think anything of that.' His eyes held Miss Pink's. 'It's a somewhat irregular household. He'd locked up but she had a key, of course. She takes—took—sleeping pills and was a late riser. They had separate rooms and when the doctor and I arrived on Saturday morning after finding the body, he didn't even know she was missing.'

'Who gave you all these details?' Miss Pink asked, merely for the record; she was a countrywoman.

'It gets around, and the police have questioned most, if not all of us.'

Miss Pink regarded him with a singular lack of expression. Arabella, who had been dying to interrupt, succeeded. 'But you said you asked Miss Pink to come here to see if she could trace the sheep. Peta's murder can't have anything to do with that!'

Rumney said heavily, 'Mossop's got a cattle wagon, and very good dogs. You know Sheepbone Moss?' Miss Pink signified that she did. 'Our sheep go up by Gathering Hill and right along the watershed above Rannerdale; they can—and do—go as far as the pass at Whirl Howe. You could bring them down off Whirl Howe and into a wagon hidden in the forest below the pass.'

'What makes you suspect this Mossop?'

'Apart from his knowing the fells and sheep—he's got a few himself—he's dishonest. He was up in court last week: stolen whisky was found on his premises. I don't necessarily suspect Mossop; it's just that whoever's stealing our sheep knows our fells. I can't think of any of our neighbours I dislike as much as Mossop.'

Miss Pink considered this. 'You think there is a connection?'

'I've had a curious letter.' Even his mother evinced interest as he extracted it from the pocket of his disreputable jacket, got up and, skirting the cats, handed it to the visitor. It was printed in regular characters on blue Basildon Bond paper and read simply:

PETA WAS GETTING ANONYMOUS LETTERS.

Miss Pink studied this and said, 'It does seem odd to receive an anonymous letter about anonymous letters; the implication being that there are two letter writers: a "good" one trying to expose an evil one? Did you keep the envelope?'

He shook his head. 'That must have been cleared away. The address was printed in the same way—it caught my eye —and the postmark was Carnthorpe.'

'Do you know anyone else who's had similar letters?'

None of them knew of anyone.

'Have the police seen this?' she asked.

'No. I reckon everything's related; sheep stealing's big business nowadays, and if Mossop was the villain, it's an odd coincidence that his wife should have been murdered. Who sent anonymous letters to her and what did they say? Who sent this letter to me? I'd rather not bring the police into it. We're a bit clannish in Sandale,' he explained, 'and sheep stealing's not the kind of thing you want noised abroad.' She nodded; she'd lived most of her life in sheep country. 'Besides,' he went on, 'suppose it isn't Mossop taking the sheep—which there's no proof of anyway, any more than there's proof of his killing his wife? They could have been stolen by some other neighbour.' He thought about this. 'That would be horrible.'

Grannie said regretfully, 'It's a great pity it couldn't be someone from outside.'

'He knows our fells too well, Mother.'

'It was right not to bring the police in.' She nodded to herself. 'We've always settled our own affairs.'

Miss Pink caught Arabella's eye. The girl said: 'Sheep stealing, murder and anonymous letters: all in one tiny dale; there must be some connection. Where do you start?'

Rumney turned to her. 'What story will you tell people to account for your being here?'

'I shall be looking for a cottage,' she said firmly. 'Is there a ruin which I might spend some time poking around?'

'There's an old barn across the beck that belongs to some people called Dalton who own Burblethwaite. They applied for planning permission to convert it but I'm not sure what the position is about that. You could go and have a look at the place and even inquire of the tenant. Burblethwaite is let to a fellow called Harper.' Arabella giggled and he went on good-humouredly, 'I must attend to Penelope. Arabella will tell you about Harper, or rather, his visitor; I daresay she'll do better at it than me.'

He went out. Miss Pink looked at Arabella and thought what an expressive little face it was, far from conventionally beautiful with its broad nose and wide mouth but interesting to watch.

'Mr Harper is a visitor from Surrey,' Grannie intoned.

'Oh, *he's* not interesting, Gran—but that's the point—' Arabella turned to Miss Pink eagerly. 'An old man—' she began, and checked herself immediately, disconcerted, 'well,

47

middle-aged, but so dull! He had to sell his business because of the economic situation and he came here for a rest. He's completely inarticulate and he doesn't do anything but potter in the garden: digging up the Daltons' bulbs and putting them back again furtively as if he'd found a grave, and going for little walks up to Dalehead—not farther because he says the mist comes down like a stone! And he's terrified out of his life of burglars. Someone tried to break in at Burblethwaite and he had all the locks changed: front and back, even the coal shed! He's got something called mortice deadlocks now.'

'They have a lot of burglaries in the south,' Grannie put in. 'He told me. He's worried about the stuff in the place.'

'Oh, Gran! An old television set and George Harper's transistor! He's so obsessed with the thought of campers breaking in, he's forgotten it's winter time and all the campers have gone home. And this is the astonishing thing—' she turned to Miss Pink with saucer eyes, 'here's this funny little guy, who's scared of his own shadow, entertaining the most marvellous person: well, what you can see of her as she goes by.... She drives a Lotus Europa—that is, she owns it; she can't drive.' She pursed her lips primly. 'It's O.K. doing a hundred on freeways if you're very beautiful, because you can't do any harm and you won't even get a ticket from the traffic cops, just a proposition if they've got the nerve, but to do fifty up Sandale lane is not on. Funny,' she mused, 'George Harper can't drive either.'

'I take it,' Miss Pink put in, 'that you mean they're bad drivers as opposed to non-drivers.'

Arabella grinned. 'I exaggerate,' she said carelessly. 'Oh, this gorgeous lady can drive after a fashion, and one can forgive a lot, that is, until she hits one of our sheep, or a person on Storms' bend.' She shuddered.

'What is her relationship to Mr Harper?'

'Oh, she couldn't be his *wife*!'

'His daughter?'

'Why, that never occurred to me. You'll think we're

obsessed with sex in Sandale, but we all thought . . . Of course, that's far more reasonable. Poor George, what would he have to attract this kind of girl? I don't mean to be rude but she is lovely and she wears the most gorgeous clothes.' She looked down at her skirt. 'No matter what I pay for an outfit, I can never look elegant. My mother does, and so does Lucy Fell; it's a matter of height. This lady at Burblethwaite is built like a racehorse: all legs and a small head and a beautiful mane of chestnut hair. I saw her walking up the outrake before they went driving this morning. She moves like a model. Probably that's what she is.'

'And how long is she here for?'

'No one knows. No one knows anything. She arrived some days ago and since then they've gone out in her car in the mornings and not come back till after dark. George creeps across for the milk and Zeke's far too gentlemanly to ask questions. I go down for the milk but I'm sure George hides round the corner until I've gone. The girl hasn't crossed the bridge to our side since she's been here, except in her car, and they never stop. And George gives a feeble grin and kind of contracts inside his sheepskin as if he's embarrassed. I guess that's why we thought it was a sexual relationship.'

'How many people are there in this hamlet?'

'Besides us and George Harper, there's Lucy Fell at Thornbarrow, and above the green there's Coneygarth which is ours and is let to a guy called Jackson Wren—' her face was momentarily blank. 'It's Lucy who's friendly with Denis Noble. He makes pet food and Zeke says he's not doing so well. He's got a house just above the Throat and his wife is an alcoholic so we don't see much of her.'

'Your uncle said Peta Mossop was drunk at Lucy Fell's house on the evening before she died. Do you know anything about that?'

'Yes, well, Zeke leaves out the best gossip so there are big gaps. Peta had an affair with Denis. I can't think why; he's old enough to be her grandfather and they'd known each

49

other for years; you wouldn't think there was much mystery left. Anyway, Lucy gave a party—in September, wasn't it Gran?—and Peta seduced Denis. After that and for several weeks they had a wild affair and then they cooled it, just like that. Denis and Lucy went away to London last week and came back and then they started their little Friday night dinners again (everyone knew about it; all very comic opera), and Peta walked in on them. Now you ask me, I don't know what the scene was about—if there was a scene. It couldn't have been anything important. Perhaps the inspector told Zeke, or Lucy did. Did he say, Gran?'

'Peta was getting telephone calls.'

'Oh those!' Arabella turned back to Miss Pink. 'She had a breakdown three years ago and she said she had telephone calls then. Afterwards she said she made it up. This was the same kind of thing.'

'How do you know?'

'Why, it must have been. It was obvious she'd gone over the edge again: imagining nasty people threatening her on the phone. She was paranoid.'

'But someone was threatening her.'

'What makes you say that?'

'Someone thought Peta was threatened,' Miss Pink elaborated, 'otherwise why write to your uncle saying so? In any case, it's logical to assume she was being threatened, since she was murdered, isn't it?'

Chapter 6

A FIRE OF coal and birch logs burned in the room allocated to Miss Pink. The little iron grate was surrounded by tiles, each painted with a different wild flower. The wallpaper featured tiny floral sprigs, and the quilt was patchwork. Rag rugs covered the floor which was composed of huge and slightly undulating planks with iron studs for nails.

She put out the light and went to the window. After some minutes her eyes became accustomed to the dark but there were no other lights visible, only the suspicion of a glimmer down on the right where, she suspected, Rumney attended Penelope.

She felt curiously at a loose end and wondered, as Arabella had wondered, where she should begin; particularly since the beginning was farther back than the finding of Peta's body. Anonymous letters were more Miss Pink's style than sheep stealing, which was really Rumney's department. The murder was a police matter; she was hardly in a position to grill people for forty-eight hours, as was supposed to have happened to Mossop. So her focal point should be the letters, or rather, the letter, for only Rumney's was a fact; if his had been written by an unstable person, then those to which it referred could well be fantasy.

She took it from her pocket. PETA WAS GETTING ANONYMOUS LETTERS. Good printing, concise and accurate. 'Anonymous' spelt correctly. The communication of a literate person and perhaps a cultured one. There appeared to be no attempt to disguise the hand, only the small gesture of capitals instead of lower case, but surely a person intelligent enough to pen this statement would guess that printing could be traced?

*   *   *

51

'Who were Peta Mossop's friends?'

In Donegal tweed and a shirt in *eau de nil*, Miss Pink sipped Tio Pepe in Rumney's office. Once the parlour, this was now utilitarian with an old rolltop desk holding letters, bills, copies of the *Farmer's Weekly* and several editions of *The Shepherd's Guide*.

'I don't know that she had any friends,' Rumney said slowly. 'The police asked who disliked her, which seems more to the point. Friends. Let's think about it. There's Noble, of course; the police questioned him for a long time, although not as long as Mossop. Noble could have felt bad about the way he'd treated her but that wouldn't make him feel friendly towards her; irritation would be more his attitude. As for Lucy Fell: she must have hated Peta; Peta was the opposition: the younger woman challenging the establishment. Jackson Wren? He had nothing to do with her.' His mouth snapped shut and Miss Pink didn't comment. After a while he took a deep breath. 'You've hit on something,' he admitted— as if she'd spoken after all, 'in fact, Wren is the real reason that I asked you to come to Sandale.' She nodded; she'd thought that the invitation was odd and that subsequent explanations kept something back. 'Wren knew my sheep were missing before I told him,' Rumney went on, 'and he was embarrassed when I picked him up on it. But that exchange occurred the moment before we came across Peta's body, and I've not mentioned it since. I wasn't happy about the situation. Arabella's keen on the fellow, d'you see. She says it's over, but you know these youngsters. . . . I'd like to think it's over, even without the sheep business, but I can't be sure. He wants to start a pony trekking centre but he's got no money; Arabella's attraction for him is financial. But there, you must judge when you see him—and perhaps Arabella will talk to you; she's very subdued over it with us. But there's something odd about Wren; he's shifty. He's a local man but he's been away from the valley for a long time. He's a drifter: one of

52

those who can turn his hand to anything, but won't; lazy and more than a bit greedy but, as I said, you must judge.'

'Short cuts are necessary sometimes,' she murmured. 'How does he come to be occupying your cottage?'

He looked rueful. 'He convinced me that he was hard-working and ambitious. He'd live there rent-free, he said, and modernise the place: put in a ring main, dig drains, build a septic tank. Eventually he would lease land from me for grazing his ponies.' Rumney shook his head. 'He's glib; that's how he fascinated Arabella: with talk, but she's got to find out about him the hard way.'

'Why haven't you given him notice to quit?'

'He's only been at Coneygarth a few months; before I'd got his measure Arabella arrived from the States and took to him immediately. If I'd sent him packing then, she'd have gone with him—Mother saw that. But he knows my patience is wearing thin, and now may be the time to do something about it except that I don't know how things stand between him and Arabella.'

'I wouldn't give him notice at the moment if I were you. So you think there might be a connection between him and Mossop where the sheep stealing's concerned?'

He didn't answer directly. 'It's very involved and un-pleasant. You see, Mossop's wife had an affair with Denis Noble, and *he* was associating with Lucy; it's all a matter of criss-crossed lines—and then Wren was the last person to see Peta alive—' He checked. 'No, I don't mean that; the killer was the last person, but Wren saw her after she left Thorn-barrow: saw her near the bottom of Storms' drive, staggering in the lane as if she were drunk.'

'What time did he see her?' She forgot that she'd thought of the murder as a police matter.

'He says some time after ten-thirty; she was just this side of Storms. He was coming home from an evening's drinking in Carnthorpe and he was alone.'

'Did the autopsy manage to come anywhere near the time of death?'

'The pathologist wouldn't commit himself but he said she was probably dead before three o'clock in the morning.'

'And Wren saw her alive at ten-thirty.'

'That's what he says. But you were asking me about her friends.'

'Did George Harper know her?'

'Not to my knowledge. I only saw them together once, and by that I mean in the same room; that was at Lucy's party in September when Peta concentrated in a rather embarrassing fashion on Noble. Why do you ask?'

'I'm trying to work through everyone—or at least, the Sandale residents. This girl who's staying at Burblethwaite: she arrived after Peta's death?'

'Yes. Peta was killed on Friday night or Saturday morning. Harper's guest arrived last Tuesday, the day of the inquest.'

She put her head on one side and blinked. Rumney thought she looked a trifle stupid and wondered if his friend Roberts had been misled concerning her abilities.

'Everyone seems to know about the affair between Noble and Peta,' she remarked. 'Did they know at the time?'

'Oh, bound to have done; you can't hide those things in a community of this size. Peta used to catch the afternoon bus to Carnthorpe and come back in the small hours. Mossop joked about it with his cronies in the bar but he didn't *name* Noble. Jackson Wren drinks at Storms, and he told Arabella what Mossop was saying. Peta must have met Noble in Carnthorpe and he would have brought her home in his car. You can't hope to hide a thing like that.'

'What was Mrs Noble's reaction?'

'I don't know.' She regarded him thoughtfully. She didn't look stupid now. 'One doesn't see much of Sarah,' he elaborated, 'I doubt if I've seen her for weeks and, frankly, I can't imagine Sarah confiding in any of us. She rambles, she talks

54

wildly at times, but she isn't the kind of alcoholic who sobs on your shoulder—oh no, Sarah can be very close.'

'And the Brights?'

'Quentin was her doctor. He's a conscientious chap; he was very upset at the inquest: a face on him like a stone. Yes, Quentin was well-disposed towards her; more, he'd feel guilty.'

'Why?'

'Why would he feel guilty? Because she was killed.'

'He'd think he failed her?'

'Just failed. Failed somewhere. He blames himself for too much that goes wrong with his patients. He's a good friend of mine.' There could have been a warning in his voice.

'Tell me where he thought he failed in this case.'

He sighed and shook his head as if to clear cobwebs. He filled their glasses from the decanter.

'There's something telepathic here,' he told her, 'because I can't give any explanation. I know he feels guilty.' He glanced at her quickly. 'You do realise I'm not referring to any form of direct guilt?'

'Of course.'

'A sin of omission,' he went on, reassured. 'Apparently Peta was hysterical when she went to Thornbarrow that Friday night, and Wren says she was weaving across the road. It's assumed she was drunk; there was quite a high level of alcohol in the blood—'

'Any barbiturates or anything like that?'

'No, why?'

'Just a point. Of elimination.'

'Quentin felt he should have kept a closer eye on her. Funny thing your asking about barbiturates; he was prescribing sleeping tablets but she wouldn't tell him the trouble. He didn't know she had a problem but he felt that she had. Of course, anyone who can't sleep has a problem: insomnia's only a symptom. He thinks he should have probed deeper, that's how I see it.'

'You're suggesting that there was a connection between the problem which was the cause of her insomnia and her death.'

'Am I? I wasn't suggesting that consciously but it could be how Quentin's mind is working.'

'Was there anything between them—an affair for example?'

'Oh no. No. She was promiscuous certainly; no one was safe from her. She even propositioned me at one time!' He looked sheepish. 'She would have tried to seduce Quentin; one accepted that she'd make a play for any fellow who crossed her path, but Quentin's life was far too full for anything like that. Besides, Amy Bright would stop it before it got off the ground—and Quentin's no Denis Noble. There, d'you see, you have a weak silly fellow who was flattered. Quentin has no vanity.'

'Was Amy Bright a friend of Peta?'

'She was affable in public, but Amy is always the same to everyone: courteous and correct—'

Beyond the closed door a telephone was ringing. It stopped and they heard the modulations of Arabella's voice. They drank sherry and after a moment the door opened and the girl looked in. She was wearing black crepe with frills at the throat and she looked like an astonished marmoset.

'Lucy Fell!' she breathed. 'She wants us to go over when we've had supper. Guess who's coming! George Harper and his lady friend!'

'He didn't say anything.' Rumney was puzzled. 'He was across for the milk and he ran back home like a scalded cat as if he couldn't leave his visitor alone for longer than two minutes.'

'Lucy must have been watching; she'll have rung Burblethwaite when the lady was on her own and she accepted for both of them. Now George has got to present her to us. And Lucy says we have to come too because the girl's going to be a bore. Can't think what she means.'

'Well, that's no reason—' Rumney started to protest, then saw a way out. 'I've got Penelope—'

'You've changed, Uncle Zeke; you're not delivering a cow in your Sunday suit.'

'I'm changing back after supper. You can go; come back and tell us all about it.'

'I shall go too,' Miss Pink said pleasantly.

'I did ask.' Arabella was eager. 'She said you were very welcome. I've prepared the ground.' She was conspiratorial.

'What did you say?' Rumney was sharp.

She sparkled at them. 'I warned her that she might find Miss Pink a bit dull too. Is that what I should have said?'

'That's fine,' Miss Pink said with approval. 'That should do very well indeed.'

Chapter 7

SUPPER WAS GAMMON baked with prunes, and a blue Cheshire and an excellent port. Miss Pink, regarding the Rumney family with additional respect, caught Arabella's eye and saw that the respect was mutual.

'Lucy fancies herself as a cook,' the girl said as they walked down to Thornbarrow. 'I'm warning you because I see you're a gourmet, and gourmets aren't dull. I guess it would be better if you were a mutton and boiled potatoes buff.'

'That would be extreme; fish pie perhaps, and parsley sauce.'

'Yuk,' said Arabella in the dark, leading the way under a gable-end and through a gateway. It was a mild night, and distant sounds, like water and a curlew's wail, were muffled, as if the cloud were down.

The girl lifted a latch and walked into the house, calling their hostess's name. Miss Pink followed, shutting the door, peering at the stone slabs in the passage, at the firelight reflected from oak and pewter in the dim main room. A woman appeared in the opposite doorway and turned on more lights.

Lucy Fell wore grey flannel: a safari jacket and a skirt flared to the ankles, and under it a white polo-necked sweater. The only colour—and it was startling—came from the rings on her large brown hands. Miss Pink was taken aback. Arabella had not prepared her for a beautiful woman, but as they made conversation and moved towards the fire, she saw that the fascination of Lucy Fell came less from good bones or fine clothes, or jewels that were fabulous for Sandale, but from a repressed excitement not only in the woman's eyes but in her voice, even in her movements. She seemed tense and fierce.

Miss Pink asked the date of the bread cupboard and

watched the other's hands. They rested tranquil in her lap. She lied smoothly concerning her own presence in the dale and Lucy said that she couldn't think of any cottages for sale right at the moment. Miss Pink asked how long she had lived here and learned that Edward Fell had been in the Army and that the Fells came here four years ago when they retired after his last spell of duty in Cyprus. He had survived retirement for only one year. Lucy agreed that it had been a tragedy.

Arabella turned the pages of *Vogue*, Miss Pink beamed at the fire and Lucy said suddenly: 'I assume they'll come.'

'You think George won't let her come?' Arabella exclaimed. 'Now why all the mystery? Why *is* he so anti-social?'

'He isn't; he had a drink with me last Friday.'

'I thought he never went out. Last Friday! Of course he did; he brought your eggs down. But that was when—'

'He looked in early, before dinner, and he was quite amiable.' Lucy smiled at Miss Pink. 'Has Arabella told you about our visitors?'

'This is the man from Surrey? Yes, she has told me. He's not such a recluse then if he visits you.'

'Of course he's not a recluse. Arabella exaggerates. George came to my party in September and mixed quite happily.'

'What I mean is—' Arabella began, but at this point there was a knock at the outside door. Lucy rose and went out. There was a sound of greetings in the passage and Arabella mimed anticipation at Miss Pink.

They weren't disappointed. The visitor from Burblethwaite had long legs and a mass of russet hair, much of it falling casually over one eye. She wore coral-coloured *lamé*: pants, smock and camisole, and gold boots. She was pretty rather than beautiful, with an expression modelled on Marilyn Monroe but with none of Monroe's blatant sex appeal. The eyes were wide and innocent, the lips not quite closed. She was ornamental rather than functional, like a *Playboy* photograph, and she acknowledged the introductions in a strong Cockney accent that was good enough to be genuine.

Behind her George Harper appeared proud and anxious at the same time. She was his daughter and her name was Caroline. She was a model. Arabella looked meaningly at Miss Pink. So far there were no great surprises, discounting the *lamé*.

Lucy served drinks. She was the type of woman which improves in the face of opposition. Arabella, with no claims to conventional beauty and no self-consciousness, was unrecognised as competition, but Caroline Harper was a rival: young and slim and strikingly dressed. Even the accent competed.

In the face of this Lucy glowed with confidence, drawing the girl out, stylishly amused, and Caroline chattered in a breathless accent while Harper listened, Miss Pink watched benignly, and Arabella appeared to withdraw, her dark little face sinking into the black frills at her throat.

Caroline said that she was leaving the next day. Lucy was shocked. 'But you've only just arrived!'

'I've got a very full week from Monday on,' Caroline explained. 'If I drive home tomorrow I can sleep all day Sunday. But I'll be down again soon if Dad'll have me.'

'Of course I will,' he assured her. 'You're always welcome; you know that.'

It was touching, even intimate; Miss Pink had the feeling that she was eavesdropping.

'Who do you model for?' Arabella asked.

Caroline hesitated. 'I'm only just starting,' she confessed, 'but I got next week off and this guy's going to do some special pictures of me for free. I'm an air hostess really but I done some modelling for mail order firms. What I really want to do is get with a Paris house, Givenchy or Bohan or one of those. I done a bit for Warners—that's just underwear and stuff, but I'd love to be with a couturier.'

'I don't think you should have any trouble,' Arabella said sincerely, her eyes on the coral suit.

'You shouldn't have hidden away while you've been here,' Lucy chided. 'We've seen nothing of you, and you're highly decorative, for Sandale.' She glanced at Arabella and grimaced. 'Although we could hardly have raised people to have a *young* party, could we?'

'Why young?' Arabella asked with hostility. 'I like people mixed. Zeke and Quentin are great fun, and Grannie comes out with the most astonishing things. . . . Sandale can make up a very good party just as it stands.' She paused, and added, 'With one or two exceptions.'

When no one else commented Caroline asked brightly: 'Who are they?'

'The drunks and the wife-beaters,' Arabella said and stopped, turning horrified eyes on Miss Pink who smiled and shook her head in disbelief.

'That's one thing you don't have in the Lake District,' she said smugly. 'The crime rate drops like a stone as soon as you leave the urban conurbations.'

'Drunks aren't criminals,' Arabella pointed out.

'All part of the same mores.' Miss Pink's eyes gleamed as she got into her stride. She and Arabella were in shadow on a sofa and now the girl felt a slight pressure on her thigh. The pernickety voice continued: 'All statistics can be read whichever way one wants to read them and I agree that crime rates may appear to be high merely because there are more convictions or, if you like, fewer people get away with it. The statistics may, in fact, only be proving that criminals are more clever in the countryside but this can't be so because there is little *evidence* of rural crime. There may be more after-hours drinking—' she shook her head reprovingly, '—but that is where it stops.' Arabella was eyeing her coldly. Miss Pink drew breath. 'Rats in close confinement have been known—'

'We had a murder last week,' Arabella said loudly, 'and

they questioned the husband for forty-eight hours, and then they questioned her lov——' She gasped and stared at Lucy who closed her eyes in mock despair.

'Arabella! No party could be a bore with you present!' She glanced calmly at Miss Pink. 'She's right; a girl was murdered last weekend and they've not yet found the person who did it.'

'Dad said she was here, in this house.' Caroline was awed.

'Yes.' Lucy addressed George Harper. 'You were here when she rang that evening; I haven't seen you since. She came along after dinner and she was quite distraught. Denis and I were the last people to speak to her, with the exception of the man who killed her, of course.'

'How do they know it was a man?' Caroline asked.

'She wasn't killed where she was found; she had to be carried there, or transported somehow. Women can't heave other women around, you know.'

'That's right.' The girl nodded eagerly. 'You try getting girls into bed when they're stoned. It's a hell of a job. Yeah, you're quite right; it must have been a man. The husband's always the first suspect,' she assured Miss Pink earnestly.

'That may be so,' Harper put in with unexpected aggressiveness. 'That doesn't mean he's always the murderer. There are plenty of vicious wives about. The police can't look farther than their noses sometimes.'

'Come off it, Dad; we was only joking.'

Miss Pink looked confused. 'Joking?'

'Not really.' Arabella sighed. 'Our murder wasn't a joke. I don't expect Lucy thought it was a joke. Didn't she give any indication, Lucy?'

'Of what, for heaven's sake? It wasn't suicide. People hardly give indications that they're going to be murdered.' Lucy's temper seemed to be not far below the surface.

'Why, of course they don't.' Caroline stared at the other girl in reproof.

Arabella opened her mouth. Miss Pink asked: 'Why was she so late?'

There was a small silence then Lucy asked: 'Late for what?'

'Dinner,' Miss Pink said, appearing a little flustered. 'Didn't you say she came in after dinner? Or didn't you invite her?'

'That's right.' Lucy sounded strained. 'She wasn't invited.'

'Then why did she come?' Arabella asked.

Lucy said, as if she had repeated it many times: 'She was drunk and hysterical; she said she was getting telephone calls and Denis suggested she should see her doctor the following day. That's all.'

'But she was killed before she could see the doctor,' Caroline pointed out, as if it were a game.

'She was killed that night,' Lucy agreed and Miss Pink's spectacles focused on her.

'So someone wanted to stop her going to the doctor.' Caroline looked round the circle in triumph. 'I like detective stories,' she explained.

George Harper nodded morosely. 'It could have been that. It was a queer business altogether; I've found it a bit upsetting.'

'I think you should come back to town with me, Dad,' Caroline said, concerned.

Lucy rose to fill people's glasses and Miss Pink followed to admire the bread cupboard at close quarters. The butterfly hinges were brought to her attention and, sadly, the place where the central shelf had deteriorated because it was sap wood, not heart wood. Miss Pink evinced sympathy. As Lucy talked, now without much animation, her eyes travelled beyond her guest and suddenly her face was suffused with that questing excitement which had been so obvious when they'd arrived. Miss Pink turned and saw a stranger in the doorway.

'You must meet my neighbour, Jackson Wren,' Lucy said.

63

The newcomer approached: a big man in breeches and a trendy jersey with a horizontal stripe across the chest. He was faintly embarrassed but when he smiled he seemed open, boyish, genuinely pleased to meet a visitor. As Miss Pink made conversation she noticed, without appearing to do so, that Arabella was watching them with consternation. At the same time George Harper observed Arabella while his daughter stared with parted lips at Wren.

Lucy brought him a whisky on the rocks. He thanked her and for a second their eyes locked. Arabella turned to Caroline. Miss Pink asked Wren if he climbed.

'I get out as often as I can,' he told her. 'At the moment we're all praying for the snow: to get some ice climbing in.'

They turned to the fire and he nodded to Arabella then stared at Caroline. Her father introduced her.

'Are you really a mountain climber?' she asked breathlessly and Arabella winced.

Wren was not in the least put out. He started to explain that he was a rock climber and there ensued one of those embarrassing conversations familiar to the initiated. Miss Pink's face was composed, Arabella looked bored, George Harper a little anxious, but that seemed to be his habitual expression. Only Wren blossomed in the warmth of adulation —which was not surprising since it was directed at him.

Lucy came looking for someone to open a bottle of wine and took Harper away. Miss Pink, regretting her recent supper, remarked to Arabella that it looked as if they were expected to eat.

'I can always eat.' Arabella stood up. 'Lucy's *canapés* are divine. I'll give her a hand.'

Harper remained in the kitchen and Miss Pink caught a glimpse of him fiddling with some gadget on the table. She looked placidly at Wren and Caroline, admired the andirons and took a reflective sip of her cognac.

'... nothing to it,' Wren was saying. 'You reach up—not at full stretch, mind—' he showed her, '—and all the holds

64

are there, waiting for you: right where you need them. It's just the same for the feet: like climbing a ladder, and the rope makes it dead safe. The leader's got you tight all the time, see; it's impossible to fall!' He stopped and studied her. 'You'd make a nice little climber,' he said casually, 'not in that gear though.'

'I've got some jeans.'

'You mean you'd like to try?'

'Well, sometime.'

'Huh! Chicken!'

'Oh no, honestly! I'd love it; it's just that I—' She bit her lip and glanced towards the kitchen, her eyes those of a naughty child, greatly daring. She leaned towards him and whispered.

Miss Pink reached for the tongs, peering at them as if through bi-focals. She had good hearing and although the whisper was beyond her, she caught his low reply.

'You'd have to wear boots.'

'I could buy those in Carnthorpe.'

'Perhaps.' He started to tell her about the Alps and avalanches and getting up before the dawn. She was enthralled.

Meanwhile Arabella was bringing plates of food to Lucy's dining table. Occasionally she glanced at the hearth but it was the look of a preoccupied housewife wondering about fuel and falling logs, without emotion. Someone shut the kitchen door and behind it a coffee-mill went into action. Miss Pink craned her neck to see what there was to eat. Wren was demonstrating a layback on the side of the settle and Caroline was spellbound.

'You'd have to wear a helmet,' he said, returning to her.

'No! Like them on telly: real climbers?'

'You'll look gorgeous in a helmet; I'll take some pictures. I've got a Leica.'

Miss Pink started to turn the pages of *Vogue* as Arabella had done earlier but she wasn't bored. On the other side of the hearth the chatter went on; like two children planning an escapade, she thought.

At length the others came in and Lucy's eyes went straight to Wren. Miss Pink saw the lids drop fractionally, then lift, but the fire had gone. Now they were basilisk eyes, flat as green slate, and they passed over Miss Pink as if she were a chair.

The Rumney kitchen was bright and warm; scrubbed clean and abandoned for the night. On a rug under the table the oldest collie thumped the floor with his tail, and the feline Bosch had separated into its units and was draped in a frieze round the Aga: true tortoiseshell, black, white, pied and marmalade.

'Come on,' Arabella said impatiently as Miss Pink admired the new design. 'We'll talk in the house.' 'House' being Cumbrian for the living room.

They were alone. Grannie had gone to bed and they'd peeped in the lighted cow-house to find Rumney half asleep on a milking stool, still waiting for Penelope.

The range was banked for the night and they drew their chairs close to its stored heat. It was Miss Pink who started the ball rolling with congratulations on Arabella's studied indiscretions at Thornbarrow.

'We didn't learn anything,' the girl pointed out.

'I did,' Miss Pink said stoutly. 'For instance, Lucy is on good terms with George Harper and, something salutory: it hadn't occurred to me that a woman wouldn't have been able to move Peta's body. That must have been a man. And it's interesting that Peta meant to see her doctor on Saturday morning.'

'Do you think she could have been killed to stop her seeing Quentin?' Miss Pink said nothing. 'Because only Denis and Lucy knew she was going to see him,' Arabella went on.

'Not necessarily; she could have told Mossop on her return,

she could have rung the doctor late that night for an appointment or merely to talk to him; he could have told his wife. . . .'

'But she didn't go back to Storms!'

'How do you know?'

'Mossop would have said! And anyone would have said if she'd told them she was going to see the doctor.'

'Would they? Do you think the killer is telling the truth?'

'Well, of course he isn't. . . . Oh, my God!' Miss Pink regarded her placidly. 'You mean: if he's one of *us* he's not telling the truth!' She was appalled. 'It can't be Quentin?'

'No?' Miss Pink asked pleasantly. 'But he could have information: of the kind that people aren't aware that they possess. What did you think of Caroline?'

Arabella pulled herself together with an effort. 'Dumb,' she said flatly, then with more animation: 'But not completely. That suit came from Dior; I know because my mother buys things there. She didn't earn that kind of money as an air hostess.'

'She said she did some part-time modelling.'

'Mail order stuff and bras! That outfit cost a heap of dollars, and *she* didn't pay for it.' After a long pause she went on carefully, 'Lucy seems to have taken up with Jackson. I've a feeling that's going to make complications in the dale.'

'This is comparatively recent?' Miss Pink's tone was light.

'Quite. As Zeke may have told you, I had a relationship, of a sort, with Jackson until last Friday. How odd: that it should have ended the day Peta was killed. I can't think of any possible connection though. That was how Jackson came to be returning from Carnthorpe alone on Friday evening. We would have been together but we had this confrontation —or rather, that day was the climax. He didn't like me breaking it off. So now Lucy's taken him in. Well, he has a superficial charm.' The tone was worldly and highly artificial.

'The charm worked on Caroline; I don't think Lucy was too pleased about that.'

'How could she be? She's old enough to be Caroline's

mother, and almost old enough for Jackson's, but she's very elegant, isn't she? Didn't you think so?'

'Very, but I thought that Jackson might be more interested in her money than in herself. As soon as a strange young girl appeared on the scene he was quick enough to transfer his attentions.'

Arabella poked the fire, heedless of its being so carefully banked. 'Jackson is only interested in Jackson. If he can get a woman to provide money, and labour, that's his ideal partner. Once he's got them, the charm wears off; in fact, he's spread so thin now, I wonder there's enough of him left to go round.'

'You've retained your sense of humour.'

'I'll survive. Grannie did warn me. You won't tell them, will you? I'd be so ashamed.'

'Of course I won't, but there's no shame attached; chalk it up to experience. You're wiser now.'

'And how! He's married to a girl in Northampton and she's got a small baby. He's supporting them.' Arabella stared at a blue flame. 'I guess some of my money went to them but so what? Poor thing; she needed it more than me, with the baby as well.'

'How did you find this out?'

'Quite simple. He wants to start pony trekking and we saw a mare that really is a little beauty, and he knows where there's a good stallion; thinking long-term, you see. So he had to have my money because he hasn't got any, but I wanted to get married; I'm a bit Puritan that way. So I said more or less: no marriage, no money, and that's when he had to tell me about his wife in Northampton—but he said he'd get a divorce and marry me. He did point out that he'd have to pay her alimony. I took a little time to consider the problem—' she regarded Miss Pink earnestly, 'but I figured that if he'd deceived me for three months, he could do it again. It was the start of the rot, you know. It's like virginity —I mean, once trust has gone, you can never go back. And there was Grannie reminding me how rich I'd be eventually and how Jackson always was a greedy boy. . . . I reckon his going straight to Lucy proves the point. He hardly knew her a week ago but now they seem to know each other quite well, wouldn't you say?'

'Oh, definitely.' But Miss Pink's mind had snagged on something else, like wool on a bramble. 'Where was Denis Noble tonight? Doesn't he usually dine with Lucy on a Friday?'

'Why, so he does. But he couldn't be there when Lucy was so obviously smitten with Jackson. When you think about it, isn't it curious that she should have a party at all? She'd have much preferred to be alone with Jackson.'

'Probably he looked in uninvited; and we weren't there for long: less than three hours. She has him to herself now, and I wouldn't like to be in his boots.'

'Because of Caroline?'

'Naturally.' Miss Pink was prim. 'He was asking for trouble. Lucy looked quite ugly when she came in from the kitchen.'

'I didn't see her face. I saw his and he looked sly; he's probably thinking he can run two women at once.'

'Only for one day. If she climbs tomorrow—and they were making arrangements to do that—she'll have to leave on Sunday.'

'That's just as well; we've had enough entanglements in the dale already; Caroline landing in the middle of it is like a cat loose in a dove-cot.'

'Cote,' Miss Pink corrected. 'I would hardly term the Sandale residents doves.'

'Agreed, unless doves have nasty private lives like chickens. Lucy is very beautiful, isn't she?'

'Most of the time. I'm surprised you didn't warn me.'

'I hadn't realised it until tonight. She's old, of course, but she has the sense to wear things that hide it. I can't help feeling sorry for her; she does like the good things of life: like clothes and jewels and going up to London often. If she gets involved with Jackson he'll cheat her terribly and Zeke says she's not well off really. I do think men are horrible. Someone,' she added darkly, 'ought to tell her.'

'In her present state of mind, and knowing you and Jackson had been so close, she would merely think you were jealous. It's obvious that she finds the situation passionately exciting —and she's middle-aged. The combination could be very unpleasant if she thought of herself as being obstructed.'

'You could say something very delicately.'

'People have to get hurt; you can't protect them.'

'I don't like seeing old people hurt, particularly when I know what it's all about.' She caught Miss Pink's doubtful eye. 'I mean, I know Jackson; you don't. Neither does Lucy. It makes me miserable.'

'Wait and see. It may all be over in a few days; these things can fizzle out as quickly as they start. Jackson may even follow Caroline to London. By this time tomorrow things could be entirely different.'

Chapter 8

OVERNIGHT THE WEATHER broke and in the morning the cloud was down to a thousand feet but as yet there was no rain. After breakfast Miss Pink left on foot for the doctor's house. At Rumney's instigation Quentin Bright had agreed to see her, though reluctantly.

She took the old packhorse track which crossed the green under Coneygarth, then rose gently to contour the oak woods above the big houses of the lower dale. She glanced at Coneygarth as she passed: an old longhouse with the barn adjoining. The bedroom windows were tightly closed and she assumed either that Wren had left already to climb with Caroline or that he was still asleep.

She opened a gate in a stone wall and the path started to mount over block scree. The rocks were covered with cushions of moss and the old oaks were twisted, their crumbling bark scurfy with lichen. Above her the slope steepened and there were glimpses of rock walls. She was traversing under the crag known as Shivery Knott and soon she crossed the beck coming out of its main gully.

At this point the trees thinned and she looked down on the chimneys of a large house. This would be the Storms Hotel. Another few hundred yards and a rash of rhododendrons proclaimed more grounds and a second house. She smelled wood-smoke. At nine-thirty she came to the third and a steep trodden way zig-zagging down to the doctor's backyard.

For all their penchant for mock-Gothic, the Victorians had a good eye for position. The Brights' house, Throstle Shaw, stood on a site some fifty feet above the water-meadows and looked up a long dale to the heart of the Central Fells. This dale was drained by a stream which joined the Sandale beck on the far side of the fields and from the confluence the river ran deep and wide and, marked by alders, to the dramatic exit from these flat bottom-lands: the rock gorge called the Throat. This was invisible from here, hidden by the lie of the land and the ubiquitous oaks. Regretting that she was not free to go to look for kingfishers, Miss Pink completed the descent to Throstle Shaw and tramped round the house to its front entrance.

'No,' Quentin Bright said brusquely, 'Peta didn't ring me that Friday night, and I know nothing about anonymous letters except that Zeke told me he'd had one. He persuaded me to see you,' he went on, 'but I don't like it.'

'I don't like delving into people's medical history either,' Miss Pink confessed. 'But she can't be hurt now, and isn't it likely that her death is connected with her past life? And then Rumney wonders if there can be a link with his sheep—'

'I can't believe that! A link between his sheep being stolen and Peta's death? It's preposterous!'

'More preposterous than her murder? There are other links: anonymous letters, for instance, and Mossop.'

'We don't know that she was getting letters.'

'True, but someone wrote to Rumney; that person wants his—or her—letter investigated. They wouldn't have written otherwise.'

Bright looked out of the window of the drawing room. 'That letter could have been the work of a disturbed person.'

'Have you seen it?' He shook his head. She handed it to him and he read the short message.

'It appears to have been written by a stable person—so far as one can tell.' He sighed. 'What do you want to know?'

'Was there a basis for threats?'

'Given her state of mind, and Mossop's nature, yes.'

'You mean someone might have threatened to tell Mossop something which his wife didn't want him to know?'

He shifted uncomfortably. 'That's about it.'

'But you'd prefer not to give the details.'

He responded at a tangent. 'Have you met Mossop? No. They had a strange relationship: unhealthy. They fought like cat and dog. He neglected her shamelessly: went off for days at a time leaving a manager to run the hotel even in the height of the season. He spoke to her in public—and of her—in a despicable way, and yet all the time he seemed proud of her—I mean, proud that she was promiscuous. Very unpleasant. But in spite of all that there was a strong mutual dependence. That breakdown of Peta's three years ago: she took an overdose, but she rang me at the penultimate moment, and with Mossop's help I managed to get the stomach washed out. He was distraught; I had the devil's own job with him. In his own way he loved her.' He considered for a moment, and added, 'Although it makes me wince to remember the way he spoke of her on other occasions.'

'Why did she take an overdose?'

'I suspect she'd had an unhappy affair; perhaps the fellow got tired of her. That was her trouble: rejection, or rather, imagining herself rejected. What made it worse that time was that she was pregnant.' He pondered this. 'Rumney says you're to be trusted,' he commented ingenuously. 'Well, once she recovered from the overdose what did she do but take herself off to a back street abortionist, and he bungled the job. She managed to get to hospital but she was lucky to survive; as it was, she could never have another child. Mossop had gone to Newcastle for a few days but she was terrified he might find out. Mossop, you see, wanted children and when they had none, he blamed it on her. Her pregnancy disproved that, but unfortunately it wasn't Mossop's child, nor could have been, she told me. So she told him she'd been in hospital to have a cyst removed and I backed her up.'

Miss Pink asked: 'Why was she so afraid of him knowing she was pregnant if he didn't mind her being promiscuous?'

'God knows! Perhaps it was that she *could* have had children had they persisted but now she felt she'd spoiled her chances. Whatever it was, she was terrified that he would throw her out, and Peta's driving need was for security. You must remember that we're not talking about an integrated person. Peta's fears were irrational.'

'Not all of them,' Miss Pink murmured. 'If she had anonymous letters, one can assume that the threats they conveyed had a basis in fact. How had she seemed recently?'

'I hadn't seen her for some weeks. The last time she consulted me she was certainly jumpy and couldn't sleep but she wouldn't tell me what the trouble was. I prescribed tranquillisers and Mogodon.'

'Do you keep your medical records locked up?'

'Why? They're in a filing cabinet in the surgery,' he went on slowly. 'That's kept locked, along with the dispensary. You're not suggesting someone got a look at her record?'

'Can I see your surgery?'

He hesitated, then conducted her across the hall to a door which he opened with a key on his ring. Miss Pink ran a practised eye down the jamb. It was unmarked.

It was the usual surgery of a country doctor: an old flat desk, a couch with a dark blanket, a filing cabinet, glazed bookcases. The window was discreetly netted across its lower half. She crossed the room and lifted the curtain.

'Your putty needs a coat of paint.'

'It's fresh; the house was broken into when we were out one day in October—' He trailed off and stared at her. She looked from him to the woods at the back of the house. 'They threw a brick,' he went on in a dull voice. 'It was lying here on the carpet.'

'Had they taken anything?'

'Nothing, and there were no prints on the window-frame. The police said that if they came in, they'd worn gloves. The first thing we thought of was the drugs but the dispensary was still locked and nothing was missing anywhere else. My wife had left her handbag on her bed but her wallet hadn't been touched. There were fourteen pounds in it.'

'Was the filing cabinet locked?'

'I don't know. Everyone was concentrating on the drugs, you see, then going round the house to see if anything was missing. We were so confused and worried. Who would have thought of the records?'

A woman put her head round the door, smiling. 'Coffee?' she asked.

He introduced his wife and they returned to the drawing room where Amy Bright said as she passed a cup of coffee to Miss Pink: 'Why would vandals be interested in medical records?' She smiled at her husband reassuringly. 'I heard you mention the records and I wondered at the time: the hole that brick made was awfully near the window-catch although the catch was closed when we got home. I wondered if anyone had actually entered the surgery but when we found nothing was missing I forgot about it.'

Amy Bright was a large placid woman with wiry hair and an open face. Miss Pink regarded her thoughtfully and asked: 'Was Peta comfortably off?'

'She hadn't a bean,' Amy said in surprise. 'She had to ask Mossop for her bus fare to Carnthorpe.'

'You can't know that,' Bright protested, then turned to Miss Pink. 'But there was no money there to pay a blackmailer; I'm sure you're on the wrong track.'

'Peta being blackmailed!' his wife exclaimed in astonishment. 'But that's quite impossible. I mean, blackmail's a long-term thing, isn't it? A matter of small regular sums, or rather, discreet sums geared to the victim's income, and kind of jollying the victim along, never pushing him too hard? But you see, Peta was hopelessly unpredictable: no money, no chance of even donating little sums, and always on the verge of hysteria—'

'My dear!' Her husband was shocked.

'But you can blackmail for reasons other than financial,' Miss Pink pointed out. 'Perhaps the blackmailer wanted something else from her—that is, if she *was* being blackmailed.

75

Since she was neurotic is it possible that she was being used in some way—a way which had nothing to do with money?'

But they looked at her in bewilderment: two rather simple nice people to whom the thought of using a human being was outside their comprehension.

Miss Pink went back to Sandale. It was eleven o'clock and a thin drizzle was falling when she knocked at the door of Thornbarrow. She shifted her feet on the damp slates and observed that there was little wind; the smoke from Harper's chimney drifted down the dale, blue against the trees.

The door opened and Lucy Fell regarded the visitor vacantly. Behind her a gramophone was playing the music from Delibes' *Sylvia*. Miss Pink beamed. 'Good morning! Coming on to rain. I hope I'm not disturbing you?' She was poised to step indoors. 'I came to thank you for a very pleasant evening.'

Lucy smiled stiffly. 'Won't you come in, Miss Pink? I was just about to have coffee. You'll join me?'

'That's very kind of you.'

'Let me take your anorak. Why, it's quite wet. . . .'

'I've been walking. I'll just take my boots off.'

'Oh, there's no need.'

Lucy turned the music low. This morning she was in fuchsia pants and a cream Guernsey. She still seemed tense but she wasn't hostile. Miss Pink heard her filling a kettle in the kitchen. When she came back to the fire she sat down facing the window.

'Did you have a good walk?'

'Passable. It was a trifle damp. Is Mr Wren at Coneygarth?'

She followed the other's gaze. The window looked up the green past Coneygarth to Shivery Knott silhouetted, softly now because of the drizzle, on the skyline.

'You've not seen him this morning?' Lucy asked.

'I hesitated to call; I thought he might still be asleep.'

The kettle started to sing and Lucy excused herself and went to the kitchen. When she returned, Miss Pink took a cup of coffee and a brandy snap and regarded her hostess benignly. 'How many anonymous letters have *you* had?' she asked.

Lucy tensed and her eyes had the flat slate stare of last night. In the silence Miss Pink thought she heard the gutters start to run.

'How many people have had them?' Lucy asked coolly.

'I don't know. It's a tragedy when this kind of thing happens: all the neighbours watching each other, and that terrible dread of the postman, and the relief when the letters are all normal. We had it in Cornwall.'

'Was the writer found?'

'Oh, yes.'

'Who was it?'

'The name would mean nothing to you; it was a sick person of course.'

'Why "of course"?'

'They always are.' Miss Pink was faintly condescending.

'Not always,' Lucy said.

'These are certainly written in a firm hand,' Miss Pink admitted, 'but not many people are totally mad; the inspiration is diseased but the graphology's normal. I see no inconsistency.'

'What I'm wondering,' Lucy was smiling, 'is who sent you the letter and what it said.'

'No one wrote to me.' Miss Pink sounded petulant. 'I've only just come here. I've been shown a letter but naturally I can't divulge its contents.'

Lucy's fingers smoothed the muscles of her throat.

'It was the work of a cultured person,' Miss Pink added.

The other sighed with exasperation. 'You've worked me into such a state of curiosity that it's almost unbearable.' She spoke as if she were humouring her elderly visitor rather than raging with inquisitiveness. 'For heavens' sake, who had a

77

letter? One of the Rumneys—or have you visited someone else this morning?'

'Peta had letters as well.'

Lucy caught her breath and her eyes were shocked. 'Are you sure?' Miss Pink nodded seriously. 'I didn't believe it,' Lucy said, 'I thought she'd made it up, as she did some telephone calls she had a long time ago: when she had a breakdown. She said she had telephone calls this time but no one thought there was anything in it. How can you know for sure? She did tell us she'd had an anonymous letter, then said she'd lost it. But you don't lose anonymous letters; you take them to the police or you burn them.' She shivered. Miss Pink looked at the fire. Lucy said, with false gaiety, 'Let's talk about something pleasant.'

But Miss Pink was not to be side-tracked. 'Peta didn't say what was in her letter?'

'No. I said, we didn't believe her. I don't believe it now.' She stared at the other defiantly.

'But there are letters going around,' Miss Pink persisted.

Lucy shrugged. 'I didn't know that until you told me. If I'd known that other people were getting letters, then I might have been more sympathetic towards Peta. Denis was inclined to believe her because he knew about mine. Possibly I was trying to deny their existence even to myself: to block them out because I found them so revolting.'

'Were your letters an attempt at blackmail?'

'Why, no; I don't think so.'

'Demands for money are usually unmistakable.'

'I had one letter; it didn't ask for money.'

'Were you threatened?'

'The whole thing was a threat. It was signed "A Watcher". That was ghastly.' She was deeply disturbed and pressed her hands over her eyes while she took several deep breaths. 'It accused me of burying a baby in the garden,' she said.

She got up and went to the table for cigarettes. The match-flame trembled. With her back to the fire she inhaled, then turned quickly, apologised and offered her guest a cigarette.

'One thinks one is so mature,' she said, sitting down again, her eyes rather wild, 'but there are some things which rip the mask away.'

'A sick person,' Miss Pink repeated.

'Of course you're right; I've been repressing it. But it makes me feel better to know that I'm not on my own. As I said, I had only one letter and that must have been all of three weeks ago; I'd tried to forget but the mornings, before the postman comes, are dreadful. How many people are getting them—and where do you come in?'

'I don't know how many victims there are. I know about it because Zeke Rumney had one.'

There was a pause as Lucy considered this. 'And what was he accused of?'

'You've got two anonymous letter writers in the dale—'

'*What!*'

'Rumney's letter said that Peta was getting anonymous letters.'

'I don't understand.'

'It's quite simple. One of the victims of the first writer wants the criminal exposed without exposing herself—or himself.'

'That's logical. Why did you come to me?'

'It could have been you who wrote to Rumney. You're a likely victim. Your way of life could upset, say, someone with a Puritan mind and then, if they were after money—' Miss Pink shrugged. It was a compliment to one who was well-favoured financially.

'No money was asked for,' Lucy repeated dully. She looked round the room and nodded slowly. 'It's all based on jealousy, isn't it? And I suppose, to that kind of mind, I do seem to flaunt my—advantages.' She looked at her rings which she wore even now, in the morning. 'I always feel they're safer on my hands,' she said apologetically, 'and I suppose I'm vain. . . . I do like the good things of life and if you've got a little money and no family, no one at all to leave it to, what do you do? Let it accumulate and watch it lose its value? It won't be long before I'm fifty, and my looks are starting to go; in five years time I won't be able to *enjoy* my money, and I'm so happy in London at the ballet and the opera and all the latest shows. . . . And I adore clothes and I don't look too bad in them; naturally I buy the best—but really, it's only my party things that are expensive. As for entertaining, plenty of people in our position eat out once a week; I can do a better meal at home on half the money. Oh, granted my friends are hard on my drinks but, so what? I give a party—I don't mean last night, that was just drinks—and I like to serve champagne —a few bottles anyway. Why not? I suppose that's thought vulgar in Sandale, but I notice no one's backward at drinking it.' Her eyes clouded. 'I wonder if some bastard was drinking my champagne that night and planning that letter at the same time?'

'What night was that?'

'My last party, in September; the time Peta got drunk and made an exhibition of herself.' She grimaced. 'She could have written the letters,' she said lightly, 'even the one to herself. It could account for the murder, couldn't it?'

Chapter 9

GEORGE HARPER WAS holding a fish slice when he opened his door, and the appearance of domesticity suited him.

'Were you preparing your lunch?' Miss Pink asked mildly, in no more mind for obstruction than she had been with Lucy.

'No, not at all. Won't you come in?' He stood back and she stepped straight into his living room. It was raining quite hard now, and the day had darkened, but Harper had his light on and a good fire going on the open hearth. It was a single-storey cottage, modernised, but with a view to only temporary use. There was a lot of shabby chintz and a smell of paraffin. Deal bookshelves held a collection of tired paperbacks and on the window-sill was the usual holiday trove of rams' skulls, bits of rock and driftwood. Harper seemed to have put no mark on the place.

'I came to ask you about your barn,' she ventured.

'The barn?'

'The building next door; it does belong to the Daltons, doesn't it?'

'Oh, the barn! Yes, I keep my car in it.'

'Rumney said the Daltons might be willing to sell, and I understand there's planning permission.'

'What's that?'

'To be converted into a house.'

'That would take some doing, wouldn't it? Why don't you offer to buy this place?'

'I didn't know it was for sale.'

'I don't know that it is, but if you want to buy a house it would save you a bomb if you bought one ready-made instead

81

of trying to make a house out of that barn. There's nothing inside: just rotting floors.'

Miss Pink looked anxious. 'Would this cottage be worth buying in your opinion?'

'That depends what they'd want for it but it's got everything; you'd never think it from the outside, would you? There's a bath and toilet, electricity, a telephone. . . . Look, I'll show you.'

He was like a proud housewife and she accompanied him through all three of the very ordinary rooms producing murmurs of admiration as he exhibited their innocuous features. The bathroom held nothing other than the usual three-piece suite except for soap and a towel but, 'Panelled', he said of the bath, drawing her attention to some bulging black hardboard. She expressed astonishment. In the bedroom hardboard had been used again for a scalloped pelmet above draped curtains in pink nylon net. 'A lady's room, really,' he told her, looking embarrassed, 'Caroline said it was a joke.' The bedclothes had been roughly pulled up under a white candlewick spread. The wardrobe door was closed and there were two suit-cases on its top. There was no dressing table but a small green chest of drawers which bore a grubby comb, a shaving mirror and a crumpled handkerchief which he crammed in his pocket.

'There's not a lot of room,' she remarked dubiously, returning to the fire.

'You can put people up in here; this settee opens out to a double bed. Caroline slept on it and she said it was very comfortable.'

'Ah yes, Caroline; where is she?'

'She left after breakfast: to go back to town.' He looked sad. 'She's all I've got; her mother died when she was five and we only had the one.' He patted a cushion absently. 'Seems a long time ago now.' His lips stretched in a smile that didn't reach his eyes. 'You've got to go on, haven't you? And I had Caroline; she's a good girl.'

'And so beautiful,' Miss Pink said warmly.

'Everyone says that. It makes me very proud.'

'Young Jackson Wren was bowled over like a rabbit.'

He shook his head vehemently. 'He'd be no good for her, that fellow; no character, nothing, not the right sort for my girl at all.'

'I don't think she was so attracted by the man as by the fact that he's a climber. It's the glamour—'

'Oh no. No. I wasn't having that.' He saw she was amused. 'I know all you people climb mountains and think nothing to it but you're experts; but my girl; it was another world to her—'

'That's the attraction,' she murmured.

'—and far too dangerous. Why, you've only got to look at her! She's not built for any rough stuff. I wasn't having her going up no rocks.... I've seen them, you know, I'm not ignorant—' he glared at her in his sincerity, 'I seen them on the telly; I'm not talking out the back of me neck. She agreed with me. I said, "You've got these pictures to pose for on Monday," I said. "How's it going to look if you're all over cuts and bruises?" I said. "You can't model nothink like that, my girl." Of course, I didn't give a damn about the modelling, did I? It was the danger I was thinking of, but when I said "bruises" that did it.' He chuckled and nodded in remembered triumph, then sobered. 'Only child, you see; you know how it is?'

Miss Pink said placatingly, 'In any case, he wasn't really a suitable person for her.'

'I've got no time for him,' he agreed firmly, then, almost unwillingly: 'Someone broke in here last night, when we was across at Mrs Fell's—'

'*No!*'

'Through the pantry window.' He opened the door to a cubby hole he hadn't shown her until now. Sure enough, there was no glass in a tiny window pane.

'Put his hand in and undid the latch,' he explained.

'Was anything stolen?'

'No; there was nothing to steal.'

'What about Caroline's things?'

'He was after money—and it wasn't the first time. It was Wren, of course; he's been hanging around the place ever since I came. If I didn't see him, I heard him in the woods; people make more noise than sheep.'

'What makes you so sure it's Wren?'

He shot a glance at her. 'I did think it was campers at first; that was back in September when someone tried to force the door and I changed all the locks. Then a week ago I caught Wren up here in the dark. I didn't like that. He said he was coming back from a walk but I'd seen him across at Coneygarth just before dusk. Then there was last night.' He smiled at her but not pleasantly. 'So it wasn't just because I think climbing's dangerous that I didn't want my girl to have anything to do with him.'

'I see. It would have been a terrible day for climbing anyway; she'd have got soaked. In fact, the best way to put people off for ever is to send them out on a day like this.'

'You don't say.' He stood at the window and looked up the dale where the headwall was hidden by rain drifting towards them. 'She'll be halfway to London now,' he remarked wistfully.

'You should report that broken window to the police.'

He shrugged. 'He won't come again: now he knows there's nothing here.'

Miles Mossop was a very different kettle of fish from Harper. Rumney had told her that on a wet Saturday she'd find few customers in the hotel bar so she snatched a bite of bread and cheese at Sandale House, then, clad in waterproofs and carrying a rucksack, she took the squelchy path across the green again. There was no change at Coneygarth, the windows still tightly closed and no smoke rising from its chimneys.

She traversed the fellside through the dripping trees and,

arriving behind Storms, slithered down the slope to its depressing backyard, trying to make allowances for the fact that anywhere must look miserable in this weather and that empty crates and dustbins must go somewhere.

She prowled round the building, peering in windows at dim interiors and plastic-covered chairs. In one room, light at the back illumined shelves of bottles. She struggled out of her over-trousers and cagoule in the porch, draped them across her rucksack and stepped into the hall. As she hesitated, a fat man appeared and regarded her sourly.

'Good afternoon.' She was pleasant but firm. 'Would you like me to remove my boots?'

'We don't have a climbers' bar.'

'Are you objecting to my footwear or my person? The boots are easily removed.'

'I'll serve you with drink.' It was projected as an insult. He could be thinking of the rule about publicans refusing drinks at their discretion but, if so, he didn't invoke it.

She put her boots outside and walked across the hall in her stockinged feet: the picture of an elderly spinster panting for a drink. She trusted that Mossop would fail to recognise a healthy glow and would put her down as a near-alcoholic.

The bar was empty. 'My name is Pink,' she announced, eyeing a high stool with a cigarette burn in the cushion and rejecting it. He grunted. 'Are you the proprietor?'

'That's right.'

'I'm staying at Sandale House.'

'And what d'you want here?'

Her glance ranged the shelves and she remembered tardily that she was a walker rained off the hill.

'Vodka and green ginger. And what will you have?'

He was an opportunist. 'I'll have a drop o' Scotch.' He served the drinks in silence while she observed the room. When Storms had been a private residence this would have been the drawing room; it looked across the gravel sweep to a wet stone parapet and the tops of trees. The ground fell

85

away very steeply to the road. The view would be the best part of the place now. Inside there were shiny brown arm-chairs, formica tables and enough Birmingham brass to stock a souvenir shop. A small stick-like object hung on a string above the counter.

'Sixty pence.'

'Your very good health.'

'Cheers.'

'What a dismal day!'

'You've got to expect it at t'back-end in Lakeland. You don't pick a good time for a holiday.'

'Actually I'm looking for a cottage to buy.'

'There's none in Sandale.'

'I would have no objection to renting on a long lease.'

'There's plenty of summer places below the Throat but they're only empty in t'winter. Folks let 'em for forty, fifty pun in t'season.'

'That's out of the question.'

'Ay, well. . . .'

'I wanted a place in Sandale; I knew it many years ago, but it's changed.'

'Lots of people about in the summer.'

'It's changed in the winter as well. People used to be so neighbourly in these remote dales; everyone was ready to lend a hand when it was needed, all so friendly . . . but now, I don't know . . . these anonymous letters going round; I'd find it very unsettling.'

He glowered. 'What—anonymous—letters?'

'Yes; it's not a thing you like people to know about, is it? Are you a victim as well?'

The glower was replaced by astonishment. 'Is Rumney getting letters?'

'Oh, he and others. Each person thinks he's the only one receiving them, and yet—how many are there? Four, five, a dozen?'

'How do *you* know?'

'People talk.'

'Who you been talking to? Who's had them?'

'I don't think it would be ethical to—'

He slammed the counter with his fist. 'I'm asking you! Who's been getting 'em?'

'Control yourself, man. You're in no position to lose your temper with a customer, nor with anyone else—'

He was suddenly wary. 'You can't be from the police—' He surveyed her clothing in confusion but wouldn't meet her eyes, 'That's mad. What are you then? You're not looking for a cottage; what d'you know about it? You're a stranger.'

Miss Pink regarded him sternly. 'My interest is in who's sending them, not in who's receiving them. Wouldn't you want to know the identity of the sender?' Her voice dropped. 'Or do you know?'

He hesitated. 'I had a phone call,' he said reluctantly. 'Just one. I took no notice and I didn't get any more.'

'Blackmail?'

He licked his lips. 'Yes.' It was drawn out; he was trying to think as he spoke and finding it difficult. 'He said as I was serving drinks after hours and said the police would get a phone call unless I left some money. To leave it outside t'back door, he said.'

'And did you?'

He grinned nastily. 'Like hell! I'm no easy touch. Besides, I don't serve drinks after hours.'

'Did you recognise the voice?'

'He were a southerner. I didn't know who it was.' Again that grin. 'He wouldn't be very fit if I had known, not now, he wouldn't.' She sipped her drink and he went on, his tone noticeably milder, 'You get these outbreaks in country districts: some old woman living alone thinks she can make some easy money on the side.'

'You said your caller was a man.'

'When did you have this phone call?'

'Well, some fellows are like old women, aren't they?'

He shrugged. 'October some time.'

'Just the one, or have you had any since?'

He looked away. 'Just the one.'

'Did you have a letter?'

'No.'

'Do you know anyone who was getting them?' She regarded him intently and he returned the stare without belligerence, considering his reply. 'No one said anything to me. The wife was supposed to be getting phone calls but if she was, she said nothing to me about them.'

There was a stamping of feet outside the entrance and men's voices. He glanced at the clock. People crowded into the hall. He went out of the door behind the bar shouting, 'You can't come in here without you take your boots off. . . .'

She reached up and took down the wooden object that hung above the counter. The string was a leather thong threaded through a hole at one end. It was about seven inches long and rounded, tapering from its head to the thong end and surprisingly heavy; weighted with lead, she guessed. She hefted it; it must be a weapon of some kind. A cosh? She licked her handkerchief and rubbed the head. The voices approached and she replaced it quickly. Walkers entered, loudly disputing who should buy the first round. Mossop appeared, she retreated from the counter and slipped away.

As she finished lacing her boots in the porch, the hall door opened and he asked roughly: '*Are* you from the police?'

'How could I be?'

'Look,' he said tensely, 'I don't know who you are, or what you want but I know that people use private detectives—if they don't want the police poking their noses into their business—' he added nastily, '—but I'm telling you straight: the police had me at the station for two days and they can't pin a thing on me because I'm clean, see? I'm not saying as I were always good to her nor as I wouldn't do murder if I found the one as did it, but *I didn't do it*! Got that?'

88

'I know you didn't,' Miss Pink said.
'Well, just remember it.'

Going down the drive she wondered how soon it would occur to him to question how she knew; he was remarkably stupid if he'd never considered that the weapon which killed his wife might be in his own hotel—or was he? She looked at the dark stain on her handkerchief where she'd rubbed the head of that strange little weapon. The police had missed it too. Could it be that, suspecting Mossop, they never dreamed that the weapon could be hanging in the bar for everyone to see, because, if Mossop had done it, he'd have disposed of it? And if Mossop had been the killer, he'd have wiped away the blood. She stopped, heedless of drops falling on her hood from the trees. Did this mean that Peta was killed at Storms, killed in the bar while her husband slept upstairs?

It wasn't impulse that made her leave Storms' drive and strike through its grounds, but the thought that Sarah Noble was an alcoholic. The Nobles were an unknown quantity; there was Denis with the elegant mistress living a mile away, and his wife who was—what? Old, plain, unmoved that her husband spent Friday nights regularly in someone else's bed? And Peta had been Noble's mistress too, for a while.

Her behaviour was deliberately repetitive. She approached High Hollins, the Nobles' house, by its backyard, walked round the side peering in at windows, stripped off her waterproofs in its porch and opened the front door. No one appeared in the dark hall.

'Is anyone here?' she fluted in the dimness.

There was a movement from the room on her right. 'Who's that?' A woman came to the doorway: a bulky little figure against the light.

'Perhaps I ought to remove my boots,' Miss Pink suggested.

'Why, dear?'

'They'll spoil your carpet.' She bent and started to untie her laces. There was no sound from the watcher. She put the boots in the porch, closed the door and advanced across the hall.

'I feel such a fool, padding about like a hippie,' she gushed, 'Now—I'm dying for a drink.'

Weak bloodshot eyes peered at her and the woman stepped back—which she was forced to do in the face of the other's confident approach.

Miss Pink entered the drawing room boldly and halted. 'Oh, I'm not dressed for the *lounge*; I thought you had a cocktail bar.'

The woman giggled. 'No bar, dear; we drink in comfort in this establishment. Sit down.'

'I don't. . . . Are you the—? No.' Her gaze took in the room. 'But this is a private house! I do beg your pardon . . . what appalling manners!' She made to retreat, her face red, but the woman barred the way.

'No, don't go. Stay and have a drink now that you're here; after all, it's what you came for. Sit down.' The tone was amused but wistful. 'The name's Noble. It's unusual to have visitors but you're very welcome.'

'I couldn't trespass—'

Sarah had crossed to the sideboard. 'Whisky, gin, brandy?'

Miss Pink gave an embarrassed little laugh. 'Well, at least I must introduce myself. My name is Pink and I'm staying at Sandale House.'

'With the Rumneys? How nice; I adore Grannie. Now, what will you have?'

'A very small brandy.'

She saw now that Sarah was a thin little person, the bulky appearance being the result of a number of sweaters worn over wide trousers. Her hair looked as if it hadn't been combed since she'd got out of bed, and as she crossed the room, intent on not spilling the contents of Miss Pink's glass, she took quick tottering steps. With her head poked forward from hunched shoulders she gave the impression of an anxious old tortoise.

The glass was half full and Miss Pink looked alarmed. 'You need this if you've been out all day,' Sarah said with a maternal air. 'Personally,' she added drily, 'I need it if I'm in all day.' There was another glass on the coffee table in front of the fire. She sat down and looked at her visitor with interest. 'My company can't be worse than Mossop's,' she remarked.

'I'm sure it isn't. Mossop?'

'The man at Storms: the hotel you must have been making for. It's next door; you came down to the wrong house, that's all.'

'I see.'

There was a pause. 'One shouldn't drink alone anyway,' Sarah said. 'It's morbid. But it's more discreet than going to pubs and making an exhibition of oneself; besides, one has to drive. . . .' She leaned forward and poked the fire. 'I'm an alcoholic; I suppose they've told you?' As Miss Pink sought for words, the other went on: 'Yes, they have. Naturally. Warned, I should have said.'

'A warning is against danger,' Miss Pink said inanely.

'Or boredom.'

'Boredom is worse than insecurity.'

'Ah, a wise woman.' Was there a hint of sarcasm in the tone? 'What are *your* vices?'

Miss Pink considered. 'Inquisitiveness.'

'Are you indulging that now? My God! You've got plenty of opportunity in this place!' When Miss Pink didn't respond, the other pressed: 'Haven't you?'

'Quite a lot.'

'Staying with Rumney, you said. Did he send you?'

'Why should he send me?'

'You tell me, dear.'

Miss Pink asked: 'Why did no one go to the police about the anonymous letters? Or just tell them when they were here investigating the murder?'

'You think there's a connection?'

'Don't you?'

91

'Yes, I do.'

'That's why you wrote to Rumney.'

'I wrote to Zeke? What makes you think that?'

'It was an educated person, and one who was almost certainly a victim herself.'

'It could have been Lucy Fell, the doctor or his wife, or my husband, or Zeke himself; even Arabella.'

Miss Pink thought this over seriously and then asked, 'Is the writer of the *other* letters an educated person?'

Sarah lit a cigarette, taking a long time about it. 'I've not had any letters myself but I've seen one. They are not very literate but they're clever—or perhaps I should say cunning.' She twisted her wedding ring. 'I understand that the person who sends them combines them with telephone calls.'

'Why?'

'Because it goes on, dear—indefinitely, and sometimes he wants the money taken to a new place.' Miss Pink held her breath. 'You didn't know that,' Sarah said.

'I didn't. How much is demanded at a time?'

'Small sums—I believe; as I said: he's cunning.'

' "He"?'

'They said it's a man.'

'When did this thing start?'

'I—' Sarah flushed. 'Some months ago: back in the summer; June, I believe.'

'How many letters did Peta have?'

'I don't know if she had any; she had the telephone calls so, since the two seem to go together, one assumes she had at least one letter to begin with.'

'Why was she being blackmailed?'

Sarah was surprised. 'But you couldn't blackmail Peta! She had no money, and he was crafty; I mean, if he only asked what he knew people could afford, he'd never try to victimise a poor person, would he?'

'Unless the blackmailer was Peta herself. Everyone agrees

that she was short of money and there's only her word for it that she was a victim.'

'But it was a man on the phone!'

'A man's *voice*. That's easily imitated. If it had been Peta that would explain why there have been no more letters or telephone calls since she was killed.' It was a guess which emerged as a statement. The other nodded, staring at the table. Miss Pink looked away and heard Sarah's voice, a careful voice: 'Have there been no more then?'

'Could you imagine her as a blackmailer?' Miss Pink asked.

The other gave this serious consideration. 'She was selfish and neurotic. Certainly she needed money but she could get that quite easily from men. My husband had a brief relationship with her, very brief.' She was objective, not bitter. 'I don't think Peta would have—could have been a blackmailer on her own; only if she'd been doing it for someone else.'

'Miles Mossop?'

'He was the only person who was close to her.'

A car drew up outside. 'You've got visitors,' Miss Pink said, without embarrassment, quite herself again.

'It's my husband, but there's no need to go.'

'I've trespassed on your hospitality for long enough—' but Denis Noble appeared in the doorway and paused at the sight of the visitor. His wife introduced them.

Noble said, 'I went out for a bit of rough shooting and got one pigeon! What a terrible afternoon it's turned out. Don't go, please; we don't have many visitors.' He retreated and Miss Pink realised that she was being studied by her hostess.

'Are you on holiday?' Sarah asked politely.

'I'm looking for a cottage.'

'Are there any in Sandale?'

'Coneygarth may be vacant soon, if Jackson Wren goes.'

'Is he going? I didn't know.'

'I think now that Arabella has terminated the affair he may be *persona non grata*.'

'I didn't know Arabella had terminated the affair. That's a

euphemism for a quarrel, I take it.' She was amused. 'We don't really know Jackson; his father's the Council roadman.'

Noble came back and went to the sideboard. 'Not the best weather for walking,' he observed, coming to the fire with a full glass, eyeing Miss Pink's breeches. 'Would you like a pair of my slippers?' She declined gracefully.

'Miss Pink says people have been getting anonymous letters, Denis.'

He grimaced. 'All over the dale, is it? That's a bad show.'

'Did you know anything, darling?'

'Well—' He stretched his legs. 'Lucy had one. Nasty thing, she burned it.' No one pressed him for details. 'Who else has been getting them?' he asked of Miss Pink.

'Peta Mossop.'

'She *had* one? She said she had but we didn't believe her.'

'Miss Pink says the letters ask for money.'

'Is that so?' He was astounded. 'Lucy didn't say anything about money. But that's criminal. No one could blackmail Peta, of course; no money there. Anyone else?'

'Zeke Rumney,' Miss Pink said.

'Zeke! How did he take it?'

'Seriously. His letter wasn't in the same vein; it was warning him that there were others.' Miss Pink caught Sarah's eye but no message was exchanged.

'Someone has their heart in the right place, but why couldn't this second chap come out in the open and say who the first one was?'

'I doubt if he knew, but he hopes that someone else will investigate and put a stop to it.'

'Bit of a tall order, that. How many people have had them: the unpleasant ones?'

'There must have been more besides Lucy and Peta, but the victims aren't likely to talk about it.'

He nodded gloomily. 'Everyone's got something to hide.'

When she left High Hollins he accompanied her to the

packhorse track. Arrived on the level he turned and faced her.

'Is Lucy being blackmailed?'

'I don't know.'

He shook his head. 'I don't like it. Who d'you think's behind it? Has Rumney any ideas?'

'Everyone's puzzled. What do you think yourself?'

'No idea.' He wasn't really listening. 'I usually go to Thornbarrow on Friday evenings,' he said with an embarrassed air, 'but she wasn't feeling too good last night. Is she worried about this business?'

'The anonymous letters?'

'Of course. What else is there?'

'Well, there's Peta's death. It must have been a great shock to both of you, so soon after you were talking to her.'

He wiped the rain out of his eyes. 'To tell you the truth, I remember very little about that night; I'd had rather too much to drink. All I'm certain about was my feeling that she must see a doctor, and if she wouldn't, then I was going to have a word with Quentin Bright myself about the state she was in. My God, we've got some neurotics in this place! Don't know what you can be thinking of us. And now there's these letters. . . . This thing has to be squashed. Wonder who it can be? What d'you think of that Harper fellow? Have you met him?'

'A harmless little man, I thought. He doesn't know anything about the countryside and he's wrapped up in his daughter. My impressions went no further than that.'

'Oh? I didn't know he had a family.'

'I find it difficult to visualise him writing anonymous letters.'

'He's not what he seems though.'

'And where would he get the knowledge of local people to blackmail them?'

'Well, he's guessing, isn't he?'

She studied the rather bovine face with the rain running down his forehead. The eyes were guileless and anxious. She remembered the broken window in Quentin Bright's surgery.

'I don't think this person's guessing. He knows.'

And there was the break-in at Harper's cottage, she thought as she walked slowly home, and there was Jackson Wren. It would appear that someone in Sandale was looking for more than medical records.

The beck coming down from Shivery Knott was in spate and the daylight was almost gone. She found her headlamp at the bottom of her rucksack and, fastening it round her head, put the battery in her pocket and surveyed the white water. It was very noisy and one could imagine that there were animals in the woods. She heard a crash from the crag above, and the sound of scree running, but then she thought it was probably the swell of a waterfall borne on a gust of air. Gritting her teeth she started to wade, feeling for the bottom with her boots. The icy water flowed over her ankles. On the other side she forced herself to sit down, empty the boots, put them on again with no wrinkles in the socks, and to lace them carefully. She stood up and squelched down the path.

There was no light in Coneygarth and she hesitated below its garden gate. She was cold, wet and exhausted. Below, the hamlet spelled warmth and comfort. The storm lantern glowed in the cow-house, metal rang on stone, there was a smell of smoke, a door closed quietly. She moved down the green; she would leave Jackson Wren until the morning.

Chapter 10

FOR HER AGE Miss Pink had excellent powers of recuperation. When she walked into the Rumney kitchen Grannie's mouth had tightened at sight of the other's drawn face. 'Fetch a glass of brandy,' she snapped at Arabella.

'No!' Miss Pink exclaimed, 'I've had too much of Sarah Noble's—but I would appreciate a cup of tea.'

She sank into a rocker, automatically removing a cat and placing it on her knee where it woke up, took one sniff at wet tweeds and leapt down. Despite her waterproofs, or because of them, she felt damp all over. She started to unlace her boots, explaining about the flooded beck. Arabella whisked away to draw a bath and came back to drive the guest upstairs.

With a tea tray on a chair beside her Miss Pink lay in a hot bath like a fox with vermin, only her mask projecting above the surface and surrounded, not by drowning fleas but a steaming cloud of Lanvin's *Arpège*.

Eventually her cerebral processes reverted to normal and by the time she descended to the living room, clean, dry and exotically perfumed, she was herself again: perceptive, relaxed and comfortable, in a burgundy suit and apricot blouse.

Rumney was in his office, the sherry and copetas at his elbow. In response to her query, he replied gravely that Penelope and her calf were well. The calf had been born in the small hours but he looked none the worse for his vigil. She sipped her sherry and recounted the events of her own day. There had been no time to talk at lunch. At the end of her report, which had not been a monologue because he interrupted occasionally for a point to be clarified, he looked at his watch, said he thought it was time to eat and asked if she would continue the discussion after supper. 'I wouldn't like you to spoil your food with business,' he said reasonably, 'and it will give me a chance to think.'

So she talked food and animals to Grannie and Arabella while Rumney sat at the head of the table functioning on two planes. Obviously he was enjoying the spiced beef because he had two helpings, obviously he appreciated his own claret, but the greater part of his attention was elsewhere. For herself, she lay fallow, stress epitomised by the difficulty of deciding between a second helping of Spotted Dog and rejection of the blue Cheshire, or abandoning the dog in favour of the cheese.

They returned to the office and Arabella brought coffee—wistfully, but she did no more than reproach them with looks. Miss Pink sent her a reassuring glance, implying that she should know all, and soon. But it was quicker this way: just she and Rumney, and perhaps safer; not an irrelevant contingency when a killer was on the loose.

Rumney served the brandy and they nursed their balloons and stared at the fire. From behind the closed door came the strains of *Iolanthe*. Arabella had discovered Gilbert and Sullivan.

'I think the Brights are right,' he ruminated, 'Peta was far more likely to be a victim than a blackmailer.' He blinked at the flames. 'And obviously it was done with the priest.'

'What priest?'

'The thing hanging in Mossop's bar with the blood on it. It's used to give the *coup de grâce* to salmon, and some incumbent at Storms brought one back from Ireland. She was killed in the bar?' He said it tentatively: a question, not a statement.

'The priest suggests that. One wonders why the body wasn't left there. Mossop's lying—in part.' She paused and appeared to study some inner vision. 'If it comes to that, no one seemed completely honest, except Denis Noble—oh, and the Brights?' Her voice rose. She could have forgotten that the doctor was Rumney's friend.

'Who was lying?'

'Well, not quite lying. There were contradictions. Lucy for

98

instance suggested that Peta was the blackmailer but I think that was more out of residual bitterness than conviction. Her attitude towards Peta appears to have been one of annoyance, like finding ants in the pantry. Suggesting that Peta wrote the letters was a good exit line; she has a strong sense of the dramatic. One feels with both her and Sarah Noble that they would prefer Peta to have been the blackmailer but their reason tells them she isn't.'

'Was Lucy being blackmailed or not?'

'She says she wasn't, that her letter was the abusive type with no demand for money. Noble bears this out and on reflection I don't think her letter did involve blackmail. She divulged its contents and you can be certain there's no body buried in Lucy Fell's garden. She's no exhibitionist, so—no body, no blackmail. There was no reason to hide the fact that someone had demanded money on a stupid assumption. Now *that* contradicts Sarah Noble who maintains that the letter writer is cunning.'

'But semi-literate.'

'It's easy enough to imitate semi-literacy if you've an ear for the spoken word and a knowledge of phonetics.'

'That should narrow the circle of suspects.'

'Not much; I'd postulated a cultured person and that's what it remains—except that the intelligence level has risen because not everyone with a high I.Q. can imitate a semi-literate writer. I doubt if Quentin Bright could.' Privately she thought that Rumney couldn't either. 'But blackmail or not, Lucy was terribly upset,' she recalled, 'she was trembling when she told me what was in her letter.'

'So there are four people who've had communications of some sort—excluding me: Lucy, but she isn't being black-mailed, Mossop who said that someone tried it on; then Sarah knows someone who's getting demands for money, but as for Peta: blackmail, but not for money?'

She hadn't divulged Peta's secret, nor had he asked. 'It could be that someone was threatening to expose her unless she performed some action, or refrained from doing something. Could she have criminal knowledge of some local person?'

'I can't think of anyone other than Mossop.'

'And you've no proof against him.'

'Proof! When the magistrates—ah, you're thinking of the sheep stealing, but I was thinking of the crate of Scotch. I reckon his telephone call related to something more criminal than after-hours drinking. It could have been about stolen whisky and when he didn't pay up, the blackmailer called his bluff. The police had a tip about that whisky; they were told to look in Mossop's cellar.'

'Who would know it was there?'

'Not that so much; who'd know it was stolen? It must have been someone close to him: a waiter perhaps, someone he'd sacked—but he hasn't sacked anyone since May. A southerner, he told you; his staff are almost invariably Scots or northerners.'

Miss Pink said doubtfully, 'Peta was the closest person to him.'

'But if he killed her he'd have cleaned the priest.'

They stared at each other. 'Yes,' Miss Pink said, 'we were talking about the blackmailer and suddenly we're at the murder. The crimes must be related. Either Peta was the blackmailer and Mossop the victim who turned on his tormentor and killed her—but he didn't because he didn't dispose of the weapon, or she was a victim and was killed by the blackmailer. And since Mossop didn't kill her, he wasn't the blackmailer. So the blackmailer is a third person who entered the bar after Mossop had gone to bed, and killed her, then put the priest back. Why was the body moved?'

'Why was she killed?'

'Either because she refused to comply with what was demanded of her, or because she could expose the blackmailer.'

'How did she get the message?' Rumney asked.

'What message?'

'Well, blackmailers always have a message. I suppose it was in her original letter because nothing was said on the phone.'

'*What?*'

'Hers were the kind of phone calls where nothing was said. It's an odd sort of blackmail, isn't it?'

'It is.' She was thoughtful.

'And who does Sarah know who's getting letters?'

'I think it's herself, and I think she wrote that letter to you. She knows too much about the blackmail to be talking about a friend's experiences. She wasn't drunk, you know. Her conversation was disjointed and she gave the impression of being indiscreet but I thought her an intelligent woman and, considering she's an alcoholic, she was pretty lucid this afternoon.'

'But she suggested Peta and Mossop were in it together.'

'That was wishful thinking and based on the fact that there have been no letters or phone calls since Peta's death. She gave herself away there. But if the letters and calls have stopped, I think it means merely that the criminal's lying low.'

'What did you think of Noble?'

'Too simple for the blackmailer, but he could be a killer —which was why Sarah stressed the brevity of his affair with Peta, and why Lucy Fell said the girl was only a nuisance: both throwing out a bit of protection in passing. It never seems to cross their minds that you don't consider people as suspects until you find others trying to protect them. Where was Noble when Peta was killed? He said he was very drunk at Thornbarrow. Lucy is his alibi but would she stand by him now that Jackson Wren has come into her life?'

'Noble doesn't know about Jackson?'

'I'm sure he doesn't; he's too stupid to dissemble. And nor did Sarah, although I wouldn't put it past her to lie successfully; it's so easy for people who are a bit potty to confuse the so-called normal person. When did Harper come to the dale?'

'Late in August. Why?'

101

'Noble used him as a scapegoat. He asked what I thought of him but didn't push it.'

'Someone's pushing if they broke into Burblethwaite.'

'I don't think Harper can possess anything valuable; it's his air of mystery that intrigues people—ordinary people. He's harmless, he could be someone who's had to retire from circulation for a while; he certainly hasn't a clue about country life—and he's playing a part, but who isn't? Just because he reverts to a London accent when he gets excited doesn't mean he's a villain.'

'Why this emphasis on crime?'

'There isn't really; he seems lost, as if he'd have loved to go back to London with Caroline, but couldn't.'

'So what questions would you have to ask him tomorrow after what you've learned today?'

She thought for a moment. 'None. None at all. Any mystery in his past can't relate to what's happened here.' She paused. 'He seems timid, at least in the country. He was worried about noises in the wood behind his cottage.'

'Sheep? There shouldn't be any in that bit of woodland.'

'He said it was more noise than a sheep makes.' A wave of fatigue engulfed her as she sensed the tail of some thought slip through her mind. Rumney was saying, 'Why have no letters been found? Don't you think that's odd?'

'Lucy burned hers, Peta lost the one she'd had, that could imply that it's still in existence; as for Sarah, another talk is called for with her. And Wren: I have to see him; he's the only one whom I've not talked to. Where was he today?'

'I didn't see him.'

'He didn't appear to be at Thornbarrow when I was there; all the same, the atmosphere was highly charged, sexually charged. She was excited; it might well have been that he was in the house. He had to be somewhere. Arabella is afraid that he'll bleed Lucy dry.' She gave the ghost of a smile. 'I doubt it. I imagine that some of Lucy's passion might start to wane when she saw her money dwindling.'

102

He wasn't interested in Lucy's affairs. 'What about telling the police?'

'Nothing I've discovered today is evidence.'

'There's the priest.'

'Salmon blood. Yes, I know it can be analysed, but there's nothing more than the priest. Shall we leave it for the time being, for the weekend anyway? I've a feeling the priest isn't going to disappear; someone, presumably, put it back in order to incriminate Mossop, so it will stay there until it's fulfilled that purpose. Tomorrow's Sunday. Monday morning will be time enough to think about the police.'

Chapter 11

'WHAT HAPPENED IN June?' Grannie repeated at the breakfast table. 'We had no rain and the hay was poor.'

'Can you remember anything happening at High Hollins?' Miss Pink pressed.

'To the Nobles?' The old lady was reflective, not curious. 'At that time Denis wasn't friendly with Peta, that came later; as for Sarah, what could have happened to her in June?'

'Miss Pink's asking you, Mother; you hear all the gossip.'

'How can I? I don't get about.'

'You pluck it off the wind,' Arabella said softly.

'And Sarah Noble doesn't visit me any more,' Grannie was saying, 'I've known that woman all her life and she was always careful of herself.'

'Careful?' Arabella was puzzled.

'The drinking was sent.' The old lady was ambiguous. 'But it must be a great help.' Her granddaughter raised her eyebrows at Miss Pink. 'I would never have allowed your father to behave like Denis Noble,' Grannie told her son sternly. Rumney concentrated on his bacon and eggs, unmoved. 'She takes care of herself,' she repeated. 'Always did; you never see Sarah Noble driving after midday.'

'Because she's drunk by then.' Arabella stated a fact, neutrally. 'What's she afraid of: damaging herself or her car, or someone else?'

'She doesn't drive to town,' Rumney put in, 'but she comes to see you, Mother, and our lane's a dangerous place in summer.'

'She doesn't come here,' Grannie contradicted.

'Mother! Sarah comes up for a crack with you almost every week.'

104

The old lady looked mischievous. 'You're getting old, son; you don't notice time passing. Sarah Noble hasn't been in this house for weeks. She won't drive to visit me and she won't come through the woods because she's not steady enough on her feet. We visit in the afternoons here,' she explained to Miss Pink.

'She used to visit you regularly?'

'About once a week, as Zeke said.'

'So she was still coming in June?'

'Yes, she wasn't drinking so bad in June; she couldn't have been—but when you took me to Storms that weekend, son, when your cousin Randolph was with us, I hadn't seen her for quite a while. She apologised; it was then she told me she wouldn't drive her motor car when she'd been drinking, so I knew the drinking was getting worse.'

Arabella was studying Miss Pink's face. She turned to her uncle. 'When was cousin Randolph here?'

'October.'

Arabella poured herself some coffee. 'Perhaps something happened to Sarah in July or August,' she said idly.

'Nothing, or she'd have told me.'

'If she visited you.'

'Oh, she was here in August; that was when we had the sudden storm and the wall crept at Striking Knife.'

'That's a field halfway down the lane,' Zeke explained. 'She's right; traffic couldn't get through till the Council cleared the rocks and got the bank built up again.'

'She didn't come that week,' Grannie said calmly. 'She stopped soon after that.'

Her listeners were silent, September in their minds. September and blackmail—for, although Miss Pink had gone up early last night, Rumney had told her he would say something to Arabella. They were a very close family; he would have told his mother too but she'd already gone to bed. This morning she had said to Miss Pink, as if the observation explained her lack of curiosity: 'I'll wait till you can tell me about our sheep.' Nevertheless, Miss Pink wondered about the extent of the old lady's knowledge, and regretted the other's advanced age. It was not that one had to exercise compassion towards them in their frailties; on the contrary, their resistance to questioning could be unassailable. Old people, she thought, smiling vaguely at the table cloth, were rock-hard.

'The hiker was killed in September,' Grannie said.

'Which one?' Rumney asked in bewilderment. In the hills death was usually associated with climbing accidents.

'The one at Storms' bend.'

It was late when Miss Pink left Sandale House but before she got out her car to drive to High Hollins she remembered that there was something to do first. If Sarah Noble were involved, however unwillingly, with a criminal, Jackson Wren was a possible candidate.

Coneygarth appeared not to have changed since yesterday morning, its door and windows were closed, its chimneys smokeless. She climbed the high steps to the gate and went up the slate path. It had stopped raining for the moment but everywhere there was the sound of water: dripping gutters and down-pipes, and the chatter of innumerable runnels in the wood as the hillside drained, while behind her the beck, which one could have waded on Friday, roared down the dale like a glacier torrent, confined between its banks but safe only to that extent. Anyone who fell in wouldn't stand a chance.

Coneygarth's front door appeared to give access to the cow-house rather than the cottage but it was of good quality wood with a Yale lock; this would be the cross-passage customary in old longhouses, giving on to both barn and house once one were inside. There was no bell or knocker so she beat on the door with her fist. The sound was puny against the continuous background of rushing water.

To her left were split doors which would open directly into the byre. She moved along and saw that they were

106

unsecured except by the wooden latch lifted by poking a finger through the hole in the upper half-door. Yet solid staples were secured to door and jamb. There was a raw gash in the wood and on the grass at her feet lay a padlock and chain, the padlock still locked, the chain broken. The weakest link, she thought, and lifted the latch.

Daylight showed her the byre with tyings for cows on each side. At the end on the right was the way through to the cross-passage with, opposite, an open door giving access to the house. She stood on the threshold and shouted for Wren. In the silence that followed she heard rats scamper over bare boards.

The house was dark. She found a switch and the light showed her an untidy and untenanted living room with the curtains drawn over the windows. She crossed it and hesitated in front of a closed door. Shouting again was only a ritual. She swallowed unhappily, braced herself and pushed the door open. It swung inwards silently, revealing a parlour with the curtains undrawn. It was empty except for a couple of easy chairs, and climbing equipment strewn about the floor.

At the back of the living room was a stone staircase. She sighed heavily and mounted the steps which spiralled round to emerge in another dim space. Her hand crept up, feeling for the switch.

The light came on and showed her one large room with an unmade double bed. There was a wardrobe with open doors, clothes on hangers and, apart from an old-fashioned washstand, that was all. She looked under the bed. Dust and a pair of men's sandals.

The ceiling sloped, so there was no loft. The cow-house had a loft. There was no ladder but she muscled up with some difficulty from the side of a stall. Light showed round the edges of a shuttered window in the gable end. She worked her way across to it carefully, feeling for rotten boards. It opened with ease to reveal a few stalks of hay and crumbs of rubble. Coneygarth was as unoccupied as it appeared from outside.

Rumney was puzzled. He stood at the cow-house door and fingered the broken chain. 'It looks like a break-in,' he said, 'but it could just as well be Jackson: come back last night and forgotten his front door key. I had a spare, but if he came back late, he wouldn't like to wake us up.'

They looked across the hamlet. Lucy's chimney smoked but not Harper's.

'This door's definitely been forced,' he went on. 'I didn't hear his van come back last night, nor leave this morning, but then the beck's making a fair noise.'

'Perhaps he's down at Thornbarrow. Lucy's almost certain to know where he is.'

'If he's at Thornbarrow, where's his van?'

Arabella came up the garden path. 'Has someone broken in?' She'd been in the kitchen when Miss Pink went back to tell Rumney.

'Looks like it,' her uncle said. 'Would you know if anything had been taken?'

'He had a transistor—'

'That's still here.'

'And all his climbing gear.'

'There's a lot of equipment in the parlour,' Miss Pink told her, 'valuable stuff too: ironmongery and a new rope.'

'It wasn't a climber,' Arabella said firmly. 'A new rope would be the first thing to go.'

Rumney looked at Miss Pink doubtfully. 'Perhaps you'd better see Lucy. I won't come; I might complicate things.'

In the cold daylight Lucy looked her age but she was still elegant and courteous, if surprised. 'Jackson?' she repeated, ushering Miss Pink into the house, 'I haven't seen him since you were here: Friday night.'

'Not *seen* him? Even in the distance?'

'No.' The other bit her lip and looked out of the window. 'I thought it a bit odd myself—'

Miss Pink did not appear to be waiting for the end of the sentence. She regarded the bread cupboard thoughtfully. 'Climbing, I suppose.' She turned to Lucy. 'You don't think—?'

'Oh, *no*!'

They stared at each other.

'Does he climb alone?'

'Sometimes,' Lucy said slowly. 'When did he go?'

'I didn't see him after Friday. Didn't you hear him leave? I mean, hear his engine?'

'I didn't hear him drive away yesterday—or did I?' She thought about it. 'When you're used to hearing things, it's difficult to remember. My God! It's so easy to slip . . . and all that rain yesterday. His van! That's what we have to find.'

'We don't know that he went climbing,' Miss Pink said reasonably, 'he might merely be visiting over the weekend.'

Lucy's face blossomed in relief. 'Of course! That'll be it. He's gone—oh, to Wales or—or Scotland—anywhere. He could be anywhere, couldn't he?'

'It's those bloody sheep,' Rumney said viciously. 'He's cleared out; you must have said something Friday evening.'

'I don't think I said anything about the sheep.' Miss Pink was calm.

They were back in Sandale's kitchen. 'You didn't say anything, Miss Pink,' Arabella assured her. 'The sheep weren't mentioned that evening, not at Thornbarrow.'

'I've suddenly remembered,' Rumney said in wonder. 'I mentioned to Harper that some were missing when he was across for the milk. I'd forgotten him. And he took Lucy's eggs down to her.' He stared at Miss Pink in consternation. 'So Wren knowing they'd gone didn't necessarily mean he'd taken them.'

'If his disappearance doesn't have anything to do with the

109

sheep, what's the next most likely explanation?' asked Miss Pink.

'Perhaps he's gone off with George Harper's daughter,' Grannie put in comfortably and they turned to her in astonishment.

Arabella's face was blank. 'That's it,' she agreed coldly, 'he's gone with Caroline; I wonder Lucy didn't think of that. It's obvious.'

'He took his van,' Rumney said. 'He parks it on the green.'

Arabella said in the same cold voice: 'He'll have left that in Carnthorpe and gone to London in Caroline's car: more sporting.' Miss Pink's heart bled for her.

'He's well out of our lives,' Grannie said.

'He has to come back for his possessions,' Miss Pink pointed out.

'Oh, he'll come back,' Arabella assured her. 'There's Lucy, you see. He'll tell her he's been to Scotland.'

'So who broke into Coneygarth?' Rumney asked.

'Why, he did: on Friday night, not last night; he'd forgotten the front door key.'

'And went away Saturday morning and left all that valuable gear lying around? I'm bolting and chaining that cottage this morning or we'll have vandals in and the place on fire.'

'I don't like it,' he told Miss Pink as they went out to her car. 'If he broke in himself, he only had to put the chain back, using different links; it was long enough. And he had the key of the padlock.' He stared up the dale. 'Those sheep worry me. Of course it couldn't have been Wren; he has no dogs, no wagon, nothing.' He turned to her. 'In fact, he had no experience of shepherding. He helped me a bit but it was only a matter of opening gates, that type of thing.'

'Perhaps it was that type of thing for Mossop: opening gates, putting up the tailboard of a cattle truck?'

He nodded slowly. 'What d'you say to going along to Storms and tackling him now?'

110

'He'll stall.'

He looked up at Coneygarth. 'Yesterday he was lying to you and you didn't ask him about my sheep. Let's do a Box and Cox act and see if that'll soften him up a bit.'

'It's only eleven o'clock; he won't be open.'

'He'll be open for us.'

There was a red Aston Martin on the gravel sweep in front of the hotel.

'Is that what he runs?' Miss Pink asked, switching off her ignition.

'Oh no; he's got a Citroen Safari.'

She glanced inside the other car but it gave no clue to its owner.

The curtains at the window on the right of the entrance —the cocktail bar—were still drawn; there was a gap at the side where they didn't meet. Someone had been stinting on material. The front door was closed but not locked. As they entered the hall, Mossop came down the stairs. Their appearance seemed to worry him.

'The—the bar's closed,' he stammered.

'We'll go in there all the same.' Rumney strode across the room where the only light came from the gap in the curtains, and pulled them back. The priest still hung above the counter and Miss Pink noticed that the carpet was black, or very dark blue: a colour that wouldn't show the dirt—or blood. She had been wondering about that.

Mossop had entered by the door behind the bar. 'You want a drink?' he asked.

'Why? Are you serving?' she asked in surprise.

'I'll give you a drink. I mean—' there was a trace of belligerence in him now, '—you shouldn't—I shouldn't do it; we're not open till twelve. It's Sunday,' he added lamely.

'Where's Jackson Wren?' Rumney asked.

Belligerence was replaced by blank astonishment, then

111

something approaching relief. Mossop wiped the counter carefully. 'Wren? I haven't seen him.'

'Where would he go?' Rumney snapped.

'How the hell would I know?'

'Where didst tha sell my sheep?'

Mossop's eyes wandered. 'Your sheep?' he repeated stupidly, 'what about your sheep?'

'Tha put t'wagon in t'forest an' brought 'em down Whirl Howe!'

'But someone saw it,' Miss Pink put in.

'No, not me.' Mossop's voice was low. 'You've got t'wrong chap. Not me. Keep your voice down, Zeke; I've got residents. Shut that door.'

He closed his own door. Miss Pink shut the other and came back. 'Peta was killed in here,' she said to Mossop conversationally.

His hand came up as if to hide his expression then he drew it down his face slowly, staring sideways at the closed door. He shook his head helplessly.

'You found her.' Miss Pink was implacable.

'I didn't kill her. I swear it—I didn't—'

'No; you didn't kill her.' She held his eyes. 'You found her dead and took her down to the road.'

'I couldna' tell t'police; they'd never believe it!' There was a flicker in the terrified eyes. 'How did you know?'

'What time did you find her?'

He hesitated, cast a glance at the expressionless Rumney and muttered, 'About two o'clock.' They waited. 'I got up to go to t'toilet,' he whispered, 'and her bedroom door were open so I looked inside. She hadn't come to bed. I come downstairs and found her like you said. . . .'

'I'm sorry,' Miss Pink said. 'Would you mind telling us about it?'

'Nothing to tell. She were lying on t'floor, fallen off her chair and t'chair turned over. Her glass were on t'carpet there,

112

not broken. They'd come in through t'front door; it were unlocked. I'd locked it after she come in.'

'After Peta came in?'

'O' course.'

'What time did she come in?'

He thought about it. 'I don't know.' He sounded infinitely weary. 'Near eleven, I expect. I were having an early night and just going up when she come in.'

'What did she say?'

'She said she'd have a drink and go to bed.'

'What did you do?'

'I went to bed then.'

'She said nothing else to you, or you to her?'

'I told her to remember to put t'lights out, that's all. Oh, I'd have said to watch her cigarette. That's probably why I come downstairs; she left cigarettes burning everywhere.'

'But since she hadn't gone to bed, you knew she must still be down here.'

'That's right, but she were on sleeping pills; she could fall asleep anywhere. Cigarette could be burning and set t'whole place afire.'

'Was the weapon beside her?'

'No; he must have took it with him.'

'So what did you do?'

'You know that. What else could I do but take her down to t'road?'

'You could have called the police.'

He shook his head. 'They got to have someone for it, haven't they? They thought it were me before; what will they say when they hear t'truth?'

'You're going to be all right. At least,' she amended, 'you won't be convicted of—the other thing.' He didn't seem to understand. 'Did she know that you were being blackmailed?'

'No.' He wasn't concentrating on her. He was listening. 'It's not nice, having that door shut,' he said. Rumney was regarding him intently. 'Look, Zeke,' he implored, 'I don't know

113

nothing about t'sheep; there's wagons stealing sheep at night all up t'motorway, and tha knows it. Why pick on me? One crate of Scotch and everything that happens within fifty miles of this place will be me from now on, won't it?'

Rumney said, 'If I had proof—'

The door opened quietly and a stranger looked in, glancing from them to Mossop. 'Good morning. Is the bar open already?' He approached the counter, smiling diffidently at Miss Pink. 'I'll have a gin and Italian, landlord.'

He was middle-aged with florid but aquiline features, dark eyes and very thick iron-grey hair, cut short and curling close to his scalp. He spoke with a trace of accent which Miss Pink could not identify but which she thought was not European. He was short and powerful with wide shoulders and narrow hips flattered by a beautifully tailored grey suit and navy silk shirt. His shoes were hand-made and when he paid for his drink there was a glimpse of a thin gold watch on a crocodile strap.

Mossop looked at the man's eyes. 'This is Mr Cole,' he said warily, 'Miss Pink and Mr Rumney.'

'Not *Ezekiel* Rumney?' He was delighted. 'From Sandale House? But this is splendid! I have to see you. At your convenience, of course.'

Rumney, who was used to meeting all kinds of people, particularly in the summer, was not surprised, only a trifle disconcerted, but that was because his mind was still on sheep.

'I'm a photo-journalist.' The man produced a card and handed it to Miss Pink. 'Environmental. I'm working for the David Ramet Institute of Environmental Studies.' He paused, raised his eyebrows at her but she was reading the card which said: 'Daniel S. Cole. Photo-journalist'. There was a Hampstead address and telephone number. 'You've never heard of it,' he said politely, 'no one has; it's an American organisation and they commission books on conservation: beautiful productions on rain forests, vanishing apes, the Danube marshes—you know the kind of thing: very lavish, superb pictures, printed in Italy.' He coughed delicately. 'I'm only the small fry, of course.'

'What's brought you to Sandale?' Rumney asked.

'Vernacular architecture, sir!' His face lit up with enthusiasm, and gold fillings flashed. Miss Pink's brain worried away at the accent: Egyptian? Syrian?

'... not concerned only with externals,' he was babbling on, 'but interiors too: spice cupboards, stone stairways, spinning galleries.'

'You've come to the wrong place,' Rumney told him, 'the spinning galleries are at Hartsop.'

'I'll go there too. But Sandale House is seventeenth century, isn't it?'

'And Thornbarrow. That's next door. Then there's—' Rumney glanced at Miss Pink.

'Yes?' Cole hung on the other's words.

'A longhouse.'

'Not a *longhouse*! Unspoiled? No picture windows or central heating, an open fire?'

'It's got an iron cooking range.'

'Well, they have their own charm.' He was disappointed but he rallied. 'When can I see these places? I may see them, mayn't I?'

Rumney nodded glumly. Cole sensed a lack of enthusiasm and turned to Miss Pink as an ally. 'It's the epitome of Lakeland,' he insisted, 'the low flat fields, the stone walls, woods, mountains. . . . Mr Mossop says there are mountains when the mist rises.' He glanced out of the window at the rain driving down the valley again. 'Oh dear, there's no *light*.'

'How long are you staying?' Miss Pink asked.

'That's immaterial, dear lady; my employers are very rich.' His gaze sharpened as he turned back to the window. 'Some sun, and drifting rain showers . . . the grass is still green . . . those grey rocks. . . . Would you care to see some of my work?' He was poised to dart away: not a light man but highly mobile.

115

'I'd like to, but—' as he made a movement, '—I have a call to make. Later today perhaps?'

Rumney and Miss Pink drove away from Storms in silence. It was she who spoke first.

'Do I run you back to Sandale—or—?' She drew to a halt in the drive out of sight of the hotel.

'Or what?'

She turned and looked at him. 'The police?'

He considered. 'What would they do?'

'Look for the killer.'

'They're supposed to be doing that now. Would they thank you if you told them this story? You're basing the theory of Peta being killed in the bar on the priest and that gap in the curtains: that someone saw her drinking alone and persuaded her to open the front door. Won't the police be working on that line, now that they've let Mossop go?'

'The police don't know that she was killed in the bar. I'm afraid that if we go to them, they'll pull Mossop in again.'

'And you think he didn't do it.'

'He wouldn't have left the priest there, Zeke; at least he'd have wiped it.'

'Won't the police think that way?'

They regarded each other. 'All right,' she said heavily, 'we'll leave it for the moment, but are other people at risk?'

'Mossop's fairly safe with Mr Cole around.' He snorted. 'A formidable fellow, that; what did you make of him?'

'Where does he come from? What's his accent?'

'Greek? Rumanian?'

'Farther away than that. It's an odd coincidence that he should show up at this moment. He could have come here with an entirely different assignment from what he claims.'

'What's that?'

'Why, the murder. An illustrated feature on the murder of a girl in a remote Lakeland dale would go down well with *Paris-Match* or *Oggi*.'

'But he'd never stay with Mossop!'

'Where else?'

He shrugged. 'I'd better get back. Will you run me home? I want to get Coneygarth secured.'

As they drove up the lane he said: 'Mossop went to pieces. He must have thought over what you said yesterday and come to the conclusion that you knew a great deal more than you do. I've never seen him so rattled. It shook him rigid to see you again, didn't it? And then, your returning with me: he knew it was something important. He told you too much yesterday, he knew he didn't stand a chance of bluffing you today. You meant business. He's in an awkward position despite what you say about that priest. He could be a very subtle fellow, you know, and not a rather stupid one as you think.'

Sarah Noble was alone at High Hollins, Noble having gone next door to the Brights. He was expected back for lunch so Miss Pink hadn't much time. She declined a drink and they studied each other, the one quite gentle, the other on her guard.

Miss Pink asked: 'Have you any idea who is blackmailing you?'

Sarah answered predictably: 'What makes you think I'm being blackmailed, dear?'

'It started in September, not June, so it's been going on for two to three months. How much have you paid to date?'

Sarah looked round the room. 'A hundred pounds,' she said in a flat voice.

'Who's behind it?'

'Do you know the reason for it?'

'Yes.'

'You've got no proof.'

'Someone has.'

Sarah shuddered. Miss Pink said kindly: 'At the worst, it would be brought in as manslaughter.'

117

'How many years does that mean?'

'Three, perhaps. Extenuating circumstances would help, with a good lawyer.'

'How did you know there were extenuating circumstances?' Miss Pink said nothing. 'How much do you know?' There was a frantic gleam in her eyes as Sarah wondered if she were being bluffed.

'You hit a hiker on Storms' bend in September and he died.'

The little old face crumpled and the bloodshot eyes shifted as she thought about a drink, a cigarette, escape, until they came back to Miss Pink and Sarah started to talk, haltingly and then with relief.

'I wasn't drinking so much in the summer. God, that's an age ago! The time's been so long since. I was sinking a good bit in the evenings though, and one night, this Friday night, I was watching telly, and there was a play: about a married man and a young girl, a tart. . . . Denis was running after Peta then, you see. I didn't mind Lucy, I *like* Lucy—' she smiled weakly, '—I'm an old woman and she relieves me of responsibilities; she's a convenient fixture in our lives, and safe.' She lit a cigarette. 'But then Peta came along; she was neurotic, selfish, greedy. I was afraid he might go off with her. I thought I'd put a stop to it—suddenly, on the evening I was watching this play. I'd lost sight of the fact that he wouldn't be with Lucy on a Friday now that he was having an affair with Peta, and I phoned Lucy. I suddenly wanted him home; I wanted to have it out with him. I could make him see sense quite easily; I have the money. I rang Lucy and she said he wasn't there but he was at Storms. At the hotel! So I—' She trailed off. 'This is ghastly,' she whispered.

'Why did you take the car?'

Sarah looked at her in surprise. 'But I was too drunk to walk, dear. I took the car. You know the rest.'

'It might help if you told me.'

The other nodded. 'Three years, you said; well, it won't—

it can't be as bad as the last two months. And I might as well be hanged for a sheep as for a lamb. What a proverb for this country! So—the hiker must have been going up to Storms and he was on my side of the road with his back to me. They said afterwards that he was wearing a dark anorak and dark jeans, and my eyes aren't good at night. I saw him at the last moment and I swerved. There was a bump: far worse than hitting a sheep, more like a crash. I turned in Storms' gateway and went back and shone the headlights on him. He was quite dead. I came home to ring the police but I had to have a drink first and then I realised that no one had seen it happen, nobody knew except me. So I didn't ring them.'

'Who mended the car?'

'Mossop got rid of it for me.'

'Ah. And sold you a new one?'

'Second-hand. I paid him five hundred pounds over the cost of the one he brought back—from Newcastle.'

'What happened to the damaged car?'

'He told me they cut it up.'

'Fragmented. How soon did the blackmail start?'

'I had a letter about two weeks afterwards. It said he—the writer—was sorry about the accident—accident was spelt with two "d"s—and that I should have twenty pounds ready and he'd telephone.'

'You said it was semi-literate.'

Sarah nodded. 'The spelling was poor, and some nouns began with a capital—like "car" and "pound". He said pound in the singular. It was signed "A Watcher" with a capital "W", I remember.' Her eyes dilated.

'What was the writing like?'

'A sloping forward script difficult to read; it was all strokes. He also said I wouldn't hear from him again; I suppose he meant after I'd paid the twenty pounds. He said, "I am a lad of my word." It was vile.'

'Where was it posted?'

'I didn't look.'

119

'Have you still got it?'

'No. I lost it.'

'*Lost* it!'

'I put it in my handbag and it just disappeared. I must have burned it one night. I hated the sight of it.'

'Did you have more letters?'

'No; after that it was telephone calls: telling me when he wanted money and where to leave it.'

'Where did you leave it?'

'It was always under a cushion in the car but sometimes he changed the place where the car was to be parked; it was always a place in Carnthorpe though—one of the car parks.'

'Did you watch to see who came to the car?'

'No, dear; someone follows me to make sure I leave the car park. There's a gang of them.'

'Is that what he told you?'

'Yes. Don't you believe that?'

'How does he talk?'

'A London accent, I'd say: rather common; not like anyone round here.'

Chapter 12

ON HER WAY up Sandale's lane she met a car coming down and pulled into a passing place. The other car stopped and George Harper wound down his window. He looked as if he hadn't slept for several nights and his eyes were shocked. His mouth worked before he could speak but when he did, he sounded almost apathetic.

'I need your help. Caroline's been snatched and they want money. I suggested you, and they've agreed to it.'

'You suggested me for what?'

'To hand over the money.'

Her eyebrows rose a fraction. 'Now? In broad daylight?'

'It'll be tonight, I expect. We must go back in case the phone rings.'

She said steadily: 'You seem remarkably cool for a man whose daughter has been kidnapped.'

He nodded once. 'I've known since yesterday lunch-time; the call came through at one o'clock, not long after you left me.'

A red Aston Martin slid to a halt behind Harper's Cortina and Cole put his head out of the window, looking very dashing in a peaked leather cap.

'We meet again, Miss Pink! Will we see you this evening?' He was arch.

'I'm not sure of my commitments, Mr Cole. We'll let you pass.'

'He's going to Storms,' she told Harper, 'let him through. I'll go on to your place.'

At Burblethwaite Harper drew in behind her and they walked up the path to the front door which he unlocked. There was no fire in the living room, and the remnants of a

121

meal, including a tin which had contained baked beans, and a milk bottle were on the table. The place was cold and squalid. They didn't sit down.

He said: 'It's Jackson Wren.'

'How do you know?'

'He's missing, and you know it. I saw you over there with Rumney this morning. He must have gone with her and he's holding her somewhere.'

'Have you any idea where the telephone call came from?'

'I don't know. I've had two: a second one this morning asking for someone to drop the money; that's when I suggested you. Yesterday I thought the call came from a kiosk on a road or from a room on a busy street; there was heavy traffic in the background.'

'You don't normally have windows open in winter time. Did he have an accent?'

'Not a northern one, just ordinary.'

'Wren's got a Cumbrian accent.'

'There's more than one in it. Forget that now; I don't care who it is. We've got to get Caroline back safe. I don't *care*, I told Wren that—or whoever he is, I said I wouldn't go to the police, I wouldn't do *anything*; just give me Caroline back, I said—' He was starting to shrill.

Miss Pink interposed firmly. 'How much are they asking?'

He gulped. 'Fifty thousand.'

'You can't raise that!'

'I've got it.' He went to the bedroom and, returning with a suitcase, opened it. It was crammed with bank notes and Miss Pink had never seen so much money in her life.

'You've had that in the cottage all along?'

'Yes, that's why I had the new locks put on. We haven't got much time left; he said he'd ring about one o'clock. Will you do it?'

'The police—'

'No, *no, no*! They'll kill her if I get outside help. I've

122

promised them: that's a condition. No police, no one at all, except you.'

'Did he suggest me?'

'No, he said *someone*. I suggested you. I thought you'd help me.' He was pleading. 'Will you?'

'If it's true,' she said slowly, 'if she's really been kidnapped, then I'll do it.'

'Thank God.'

She picked up a bundle of notes. Used fivers. She held one to the light; there was the watermark and the plastic strip.

'Oh, it's real,' he said sardonically.

'Where is it to be handed over?'

'He'll tell me in this next phone message.'

She sat down. 'Was it you who broke into Coneygarth?'

'Yes. Last night.'

'Did you find anything?'

'Nothing. No trace of her. And nothing to show where he'd gone. Did you find anything?'

'No.'

He sat down facing her and for some moments they were silent, then she asked: 'How was it the money wasn't stolen on Friday night?'

He shot a quick glance at her. 'It was well hidden.'

'That's what they were after,' she mused. 'It's not your money, is it, Mr Harper?'

'It's winnings on the horses; I'm a professional punter. I've been lucky lately but you know how it is on race tracks: I ran foul of someone and I had to lie low for a while.'

'Could it not be *that* person who's got Caroline, not Wren after all?'

'Does it make any difference?' He was listless. It occurred to her that he wouldn't have slept last night. 'I don't care who's got her as long as I get her back safe.'

'It was one o'clock when you had the phone call yesterday, and she left here after breakfast. What time would that be?'

'About nine.'

'How far could she have travelled in four hours?' She calculated. 'Half an hour to Penrith, then she could have done roughly two hundred and fifty miles on the motorway. Surely she'd be almost in London by one o'clock?'

'I'm no good at distances,' he admitted miserably.

'That's assuming doing seventy all the way,' she murmured. 'Suppose she had to go more slowly? Two hundred miles would bring her level with Northampton.'

'Who knew she was coming? If Wren was with her, it's different, see? If she was alone no one would know when she left here; she didn't know herself what time she was going to leave. Why, on Friday night she arranged to climb with Wren. No, I reckon he left the dale in front of her and stopped her somewhere on the road.'

'Then his van must still be in the area; they'd hardly go away in two vehicles. I suppose she'd go willingly in the first place?' She was really asking the question of herself.

'What happened at first—'

The telephone rang and he leaped up. She followed and was beside him when he lifted the receiver.

'Harper,' he said unsteadily. He tilted the instrument towards her.

'What does she say?' A cold neutral voice came over the wire: just a voice.

'She'll do it.'

'I'll ring you tonight at eight. Repeat that.'

'You'll ring at eight—tonight at eight. Let me speak to Caroline—please will you put Caroline on? Let me talk to her.' He turned to Miss Pink, his hand clutching the receiver. 'He's rung off.'

It was true then; no one could simulate such suffering as showed in his eyes. She touched his arm and guided him to a chair, then started to look for tea things.

'Have you any brandy in the cottage?'

'I don't want a drink.' There was a pause. 'Have one yourself,' he added absent-mindedly. He said nothing else until she'd made the tea and brought him a cup, then he asked hopelessly: 'Make anything of it?'

'The call? No. Not a northerner, anyway. A trace of London, I'd say. I couldn't hear anything in the background at all.'

He drank his tea. 'The Rumneys will be wondering where you've got to.'

'Won't you come over with me?'

'How could I?'

He was right. One look at his face and they'd know something dreadful had overtaken him.

'And you . . . I can't tell Rumney?'

'Look, my girl's life is at stake!'

The Rumneys were in the kitchen, Zeke reading the *Observer*, his womenfolk putting the last touches to Sunday lunch. Apparently she hadn't been seen at Burblethwaite and they attributed her present air of constraint to Sarah Noble's troubles. Rumney followed her to the living room.

'Was it you who wondered why no anonymous letters had been found?' she asked. 'I think I know why. Sarah put hers in her handbag. If Peta did that as well, then I'd make a guess that they were both retrieved by the sender, and I think I see how he did it. It's simple really. The door at High Hollins isn't kept locked, nor the one at the hotel, of course. So far as the Nobles' place is concerned, he had only to hide in the woods, as he did at the doctor's house before he broke into the surgery. The big windows make those places like glasshouses. He'd nip into Sarah's drawing room when she went to the kitchen or the lavatory. And then Wren frequented the hotel.'

'Wren? He wrote the letters?'

'Who else? Who is left? There's Quentin Bright and his wife—but you vouch for them.' She paused and he didn't rise to the bait. 'Then there's Denis Noble. Why should he blackmail his wife and his mistresses? He could get all the money

125

he wanted legitimately from Sarah, far more than the hundred pounds she's paid to the blackmailer since September. As for Mossop, Sarah and Lucy, they are all victims. That leaves you and your family, and Wren. And the Brights.'

'And Harper.'

'Oh no, not Harper!' He was surprised at her assurance. 'He's got no drive,' she added lamely, 'his only passion is for his daughter, besides—' now she was on firmer ground, '—he just didn't have the local knowledge.'

At this point they were interrupted by Arabella to say that lunch was ready. During the meal conversation was general but Miss Pink caught a speculative look in Rumney's eye and knew that he would want to spend the afternoon in discussion. Imagining his proximity in that small warm office she panicked; she felt it would be impossible to remain silent about Caroline's disappearance all afternoon. Was there nothing she could do at least until milking time? If she shut herself in her room they would come inquiring to see if she were unwell. Almost aggressively she announced that it was essential she get some fresh air; she would go for a walk.

After lunch Rumney stood in the porch with her and sniffed the wind. She took a torch from her rucksack and put it in the pouch pocket of her cagoule.

'You're going to the caves?' he asked disapprovingly.

'What caves? I'm going up to Dalehead to look at the barn. It's cruck-framed, isn't it?'

'That's so. I thought you were going to Shivery Knott; it has a cave system, rather like the Rat Hole in Borrowdale.'

'It would be better underground than outside on a day like this,' she muttered, feeling overwhelmed by water and the noise it made, and the need to get away from him before she blurted out the whole story. 'But I'll have a brisk walk and be back for tea.'

White water was everywhere. A beck rushed down the outrake and the erstwhile pasture on the river bank was swamp. The track wound between long whalebacks of moraines where rain swept across their gravelly slopes with a sound like sleet. Far above, cloud drifted across the face of High Cat Crag.

A roof gleamed on the other side of the river: the barn which was all that was left of the former farmstead of Dalehead. The house was in ruins: two gable ends above a tumble of slates and rotted timbers.

The bridge was humped, and only the hump kept it clear of the water. Upstream of it the path climbed in zig-zags to Sheepbone Moss and Rannerdale. Water was pouring off the plateau and down the headwall in long white cascades and the noise was awe-inspiring.

She trudged across the bridge and splashed towards the barn. It was still in good condition, but no doors hung in the wide entrance on the stream side. She would have expected to find stray sheep sheltering but the structure appeared empty. The floor was composed of droppings, muddy towards the entrance, and in the mud the marks of gumboots going in but not emerging.

She stopped and stared past the great arched crucks to the farthest recesses. In places daylight showed where a slate had slipped but the afternoon was too gloomy for the holes to come anywhere near exposing the interior. Then something moved and there was a click of metal, audible because so alien in this place.

Her hand went to her pocket and found the torch. She brought it out, feeling her hand catch on the wet plastic, taking a last-ditch comfort in the weight of the heavy rubber cylinder. She pressed the knob.

A hooded figure in waterproofs stood against the end wall, its hand in its own pouch pocket and, at its feet, a bundle of what looked like clothing.

She asked coldly, 'Am I disturbing you?'

'Why, it's Miss Pink!' It was Daniel Cole. He stepped towards her exclaiming happily: 'What a romantic place to meet you again! What are you doing here?'

127

'Stretching my legs.' She wasn't impressed. She had been frightened, had summoned all her reserves to cope with the fear, and now must endure a fulsome anti-climax. 'I didn't know you were a mountaineer, Mr Cole. What's that on the ground?'

'Some old rags. Am I really a mountaineer because I got this far? That's nice; I'll dine out on that for weeks in Hampstead.' His voice changed, became businesslike. 'I want this barn; I can't say its exterior is up to much, but I must have pictures of these cruck blades. How old is the place?'

She passed him and went to the end of the building, playing her torch on the ground. Someone—hikers probably—had brought in flat stones for seats and draped them with a disgusting overcoat which might have been discarded by a tramp. She wandered round the interior; there was nothing but the trampled floor of sheep droppings, the odd and very old cigarette packet, a rusty tin or two.

'How old?' she repeated, returning to him in the doorway. 'Rumney will tell you exactly; cruck frames were used until quite late, but these look so good that they could be two or three centuries old. Have you not seen a cruck barn before?'

'No, that's why I came up here; Mossop said that there were whole tree trunks in this barn. Isn't that bridge exquisite?' He pranced out of the doorway, extracting a very expensive camera from his pouch. He took several photographs from different angles and came back. 'No good, of course; the lens will be covered with water, but one can't resist it.'

They splashed down the track: the opposite one from that by which she'd come up the dale. Cole was wearing olive waterproofs the drabness of which accounted for her not seeing him ahead on the other side of the river. Now, with the rain at their backs, they could talk more or less comfortably.

'But what are you doing?' he persisted, the dark eyes warm and intent through the water that streamed down his face.

128

'I'm taking exercise. In London people walk on commons; it's tamer there but done for the same motive.'

'I frightened you in the barn.'

'No.' She stopped and regarded him sternly. 'I frightened you.'

'Oh, you did indeed! This is a totally strange world to me; it would be weird enough without this awful rain, but with all the water and the noise and the gloom, and the complete absence of people, my nerves are at the end of their tether. And as if it wasn't horrifying to think that I'd stumbled on another body, you walk in on me with no clue as to your sex or intentions, dear lady, until you spoke. . . . You appear in the doorway: a hooded figure full of menace, and you stare straight at me as if you can see in the dark and pull out a gun.'

'I didn't—'

'At a distance, dear, that remarkably massive torch looked just like a pistol, even—with all that black rubber—like a silenced pistol, or are silencers made of rubber only on children's toys? I've seen them somewhere.'

'Why did you say another body?'

His eyes widened and he wiped water from his lashes. 'Mossop's wife being the first, of course. Or don't we talk about that in Sandale?'

Miss Pink asked carefully, although in the circumstances, and splashing through bog, little could be deduced from a tone, all concentration being on the footing: 'Has he taken you into his confidence?'

'Impossible to say,' he was objectively cheerful, 'not knowing the extent of his knowledge.'

'As a journalist you must be interested in the crime.'

He made a detour round a stretch of water-logged peat. 'Of *course* I am!' He said it as if he were confessing a misdemeanour. 'I might even be able to sell a story on it: spin-off from the main assignment.'

'Have you any theories?'

129

'Concerning the identity of the killer? None. I don't know anyone here, you see. But do you think there's a connection between the different crimes?' He regarded her earnestly. Ahead of them loomed Burblethwaite's barn and beyond it there was a light in Harper's living room.

'Which crime?' she asked.

'Extortion, blackmail—whatever you like to call it—and the murder.'

They were passing a clump of ancient yews and she stepped aside to halt under the matted branches. He came round and faced her.

'A connection between her being blackmailed and her death,' she said. He waited expectantly. 'How did you know she was being blackmailed, Mr Cole?'

His expression didn't change. 'Mossop told me.'

'How did he know?' She watched a flicker in the deep eyes shape itself into bewilderment.

'You mean,' he said slowly, '*you* knew she was being blackmailed but he didn't?' He had changed; he was still curious and alert but now she could feel a determination in him. There was no more frippery. Still holding her eye, he said: 'She was stealing from the tills and from his wallet. He didn't tell you that.' It was a statement, not a question.

'But he told you.'

'I wasn't privileged. He thinks you know already. Do you?'

'No.'

'Do you know if he killed her?'

'I don't think he did.' She found his eyes disturbing but she was not going to tell him why she thought Mossop innocent of his wife's murder. He was Press, and an unknown quantity. She regarded the stones of Harper's barn and was reminded of Caroline.

'You believe in getting other people to do your work for you, Mr Cole.'

'Conservation of resources.' It was glib but he smiled. 'I don't think he did it either. Who's short of money round here?

Who's got the evil mind?' Miss Pink's eyes were drawn to Coneygarth as if the cottage were magnetic. 'There can't be many to choose from,' Cole said.

She stepped out from the shelter of the yews and continued down the track. The doors of the barn were open and Harper was attending to the tyres of his Cortina, operating a foot pump and staring sightlessly at the rain. He focused on Miss Pink then looked incuriously at Cole. During the introductions the journalist regarded the other man with interest.

'Have you lived here long?' he asked.

'A few months.' Harper looked at Miss Pink with the eyes of a sick dog and she gave Cole no opportunity to launch into an extempore interview but led him away, making conversation.

'I'll bring you over when the sun's shining and he's in a more welcoming mood; he's had a terrible cold for days. . . . His barn's not bad; you wouldn't be interested in the house, it's been spoiled. You've seen the packhorse bridge: the parapets had to be so low because of the loads on the ponies' backs. . . .'

'Enchanting. And so is the house beyond it: those yew trees! What must it look like by moonlight? Too corny for words?' His glance slid past her shoulder. 'Someone is trying to attract our attention.'

Lucy Fell had opened her kitchen window and was leaning out to call to them but no sound could be heard above the wild rush of the river. She beckoned. Miss Pink waved acknowledgement and crossed the bridge to Thornbarrow's garden gate, Cole striding happily at her side.

'At last,' he enthused, 'I'm going to see the inside of one of these places—it is a statesman's house, isn't it?'

'A statesman was only a yeoman farmer, so all houses of this size were statesmen's.' She didn't think Lucy's summons had extended to him and, about to point this out, she hesitated. 'Just a moment, Mr Cole.'

He turned, politely eager. 'Yes?'

131

'I think it might be better if you kept to your conservation angle in this house.'

'Oh. Does she have something to do with the crime?'

Whenever he said 'crime' she wanted to shout: 'Which one?' and now her eyes wandered desperately over the dale. Where was Caroline being held? She became aware that he was waiting for an answer.

'Distantly,' she said, trying to make the words lighter than she felt, 'but someone is missing and he may have met with an accident; Mrs Fell is rather worried about that—naturally.'

He grinned and nodded. 'Boy friend?'

'In a way.' She opened the gate and went along the flags to the back door which was ajar.

'God!' Lucy exclaimed, sweeping across the living room. 'What a hell of a day; the floods will be out if it goes on like this. Who's that with you, is it Zeke? Drop your wet things in the passage and come in to the fire.'

Miss Pink made the introductions and they pussy-footed into the house. Cole stopped with a gasp at sight of the bread cupboard. 'May I?' he breathed, advancing.

'Have a look round,' Lucy said blithely on her way to the kitchen, 'it's all yours.'

He turned to Miss Pink, his hands clasped ecstatically. 'Can I see inside?' he called. 'Or shall I expose the skeleton in your cupboard?'

'What, more?' Lucy asked drily, invisible. 'You look; enjoy yourself.'

He opened the cupboards to reveal her drinks and glass-ware and, in the much larger section underneath, a collection of massive family party pieces: tureens, oval dishes for whole geese and turkeys, a complete dinner service. He ran his hands over the carving, exclaimed at the hinges, sighed over the faulty sapwood, and then stood back muttering about light, and making notes in a small book. Lucy came in with a tray and he started to plead for pictures. She treated him with indulgent amusement and said he could take photographs at

132

any time, then she released him, as if he were a small boy, to roam the house.

'I sleep in a four-poster,' she explained to Miss Pink. 'Modern mattress and electric blanket, of course, and Liberty hangings. It's over two hundred years old.' They listened to the stairs creaking as Cole ascended slowly. 'He's looking at the panelling,' Lucy said. 'Is there any news about Jackson?'

'Not to my knowledge,' Miss Pink said truthfully. 'Tell me, did you ever have a theory as to who might have written that anonymous letter to you?'

'I told you: Peta.'

'But she had one as well; hers was blackmail.'

'That's definite? That's nasty. Did she pay?'

'Yes. That was nastier. What was the relationship between Wren and Peta?'

The other was startled. 'Jackson and Peta? He drank at Storms, and probably had an affair with her—of a sort. I wouldn't expect him to be serious about it.'

'Was she possessive?'

Upstairs a cistern flushed. 'Making himself at home,' Lucy observed. 'What is he? An Iraqui?'

'Oh yes, I was forgetting you'd been in the Middle East.' Miss Pink looked at her hostess calmly. 'I thought Jackson would have been in touch with you.'

Lucy's face was stiff. 'Why?'

'Because, on Friday evening you seemed very much attached to each other and he'd know you'd be worried if he disappeared suddenly and without explanation. You *are* worried, aren't you?'

'Not so much now. I'm beginning to wonder if he went to London—with Caroline Harper.'

'Wouldn't he have let you know?'

Lucy smiled wryly. 'Not, I think, in the circumstances. She's very attractive.'

Cole reappeared, silently in his stockinged feet, and eyed

133

his hostess with awe. 'And you live—among all this—just an ordinary, everyday life!'

'Who's ordinary?' She was wearing the grey flannel suit and all her rings, and as Miss Pink watched she saw a change, not merely in the other woman's face but in the lines of her body: a softening, a relaxation, a kind of preparation as if Lucy were marshalling her forces. The eyelids drooped a little, one noticed the long thighs and slender ankles, the superlative grooming.

'Sit down,' she ordered, and lifted the tea pot. 'Tea?'

'Yes. Yes, please.' He glanced warily at Miss Pink who was waiting for him to renew his request to take pictures, but it was Lucy who, passing him a plate of scones, asked casually: 'When would be a suitable time for you?'

He flashed his gold fillings. 'Tonight?' he asked brightly, and in the same tone, correcting himself, This evening?'

'I have an engagement this evening.'

'On Sunday? What do you do on Sunday evening in this —er, community?'

'Carnthorpe and Eden Valley Naturalist's Trust are having a lecture from a lichenologist.'

'Oh no. You mean, you're interested in lichens?'

'No, in the lichenologist.'

Miss Pink rubbed her nose. Cole frowned. 'Are you serious?'

Lucy's eyes narrowed teasingly; she looked beautiful and confident and not at all middle-aged.

'What happened to Jackson Wren?' he asked.

In the silence her face went quite blank. 'How long have you been here?' she asked.

'Since last night.'

Her voice was honed. 'Hardly long enough to do a check on your gossip, leaving aside the question of etiquette in repeating it. After five years' time we might allow you to gossip about the dale, if you were amusing, but it's a lengthy initiation; anything quicker is considered rather vulgar.'

He bit his lip and blinked, then stood up. 'That slipped out. I can't ask you to forgive me; I'll just go. Thank you for the tea.'

'When you come back to take your pictures,' she said lightly, her tone halting him on his way to the door, and rising herself. 'Wear something other than wellies and waterproofs. Do you like *cordon bleu* cooking?'

'Yes.' He stood there, letting things happen to him. She put a hand on his arm. 'Tomorrow night? Shall we say six o'clock? But you'll want to come earlier for your pictures. Come any time.'

He blundered out, forgetting to say goodbye to Miss Pink and when he'd gone Lucy came back to the fire shaking her head in amusement. 'I suppose he'd pass in London but he's a bit exotic for Sandale.'

'I'm afraid I'm to blame for that *faux pas*; I told him most particularly not to mention Jackson Wren.'

'In that case he's to blame—and I'm not having a stranger sitting here drinking my tea and preening himself just because Mossop has told him I'm the local tart and who my current lovers are.'

'You did say you were interested in the lichenologist.'

Lucy grimaced. 'Double standards. I can say what I like about myself but I won't allow the same liberties to other people. Yes, I am interested in this chap tonight, and I was interested in Jackson, and I like your friend and, as I said about spending money while I can enjoy it, the same applies to men. I dread the night I go to bed alone and realise I'm indifferent to the fact. Do I shock you?'

'Not at all, but—I'm echoing Cole—what about Denis Noble?'

'Yes indeed, what about the workers, such as they are? You've met him, Miss Pink; he's everything a girl should want: rich—well, with access to money, handsome, attentive, solid.'

'Yes?'

135

'And pedestrian. We're like an old married couple. When I go to Zermatt, I go to ski, not to bumble about on the lower slopes. I have to drive his Rover over the passes for him; I want to share the driving with a fellow in a Berlinetta Boxer—before it's too late. Can you see Denis in a Ferrari?'

'He's very fond of you.'

'Oh damn, you would make it hard.'

'Perhaps, if you were a little more discreet. . . .'

'When was I not discreet? Are you a catalyst? You're the only person who's come here in years who I can talk to. Do you think Sandale is my Shangri La? Do you know why I stay here? I can live anywhere: the Canaries, Bermuda, Geneva. I've tried them all and none of them's got anything more than this place. I don't stay in the Lake District because I have a feeling for it but because I've got no feeling for anywhere else. London's all right, but overwhelming after a while; you get bloated with rich food and chatter, and you've seen all the plays and the operas and the ballets. You come home to recharge, and go back when the shows have changed and there's a new season's collections to look over. It's the same with men.'

'What did you do before you married?'

'I was an actress, not a good one; I was always second-rate. I'm the girl who never got any farther than the rung next to the top.'

'Who's responsible for that?'

'Myself, of course. I'm not an opportunist and I've got no sense of application. I'm lazy, you see, like Peta and Jackson.' She grinned engagingly. 'I like men though; you might say I've made them my career. My husband and I were quite happy, at least, he was.'

'I can believe that,' Miss Pink said, rising.

'Would you like to hear this talk on lichens? I'm sure you'd be interested.'

'I would, but I have an engagement tonight. Another time perhaps. There is one thing before I go. Could Wren have

136

written those letters? You didn't see the others, of course, but what about the one you had?'

Lucy's eyes were matt, two-dimensional; it was a moment caught in time like a fly in amber and Miss Pink thought that she would remember it for a long while. Then the other woman moved and sighed. 'When you come right down to basics, he's a worthless devil if anybody is, and he can't be hanged.' She drew another deep breath. 'Yes, he knew Peta and yes, he could have done it—all of it; he has the necessary streak of viciousness—and violence comes very easily to that type.'

Chapter 13

R UMNEY WAS MILKING and Miss Pink closed the
door of the cow-house gently behind her, not wishing to
alarm the cows. The farmer turned his head. 'Learn anything?'

'I don't like to talk here.'

'But no one would listen outside the door!' She said
nothing. 'Where's the dog?' he asked.

'I haven't seen a dog.'

He rose smoothly, removing the bucket and stool. Putting
them down behind the cow, he went to the half-door and
whistled. After a moment he said quietly to the darkness:
'Watch!' then resumed his place. 'The dog will give warning
if anyone's about. Now you can talk.'

She told him what she'd learned about Peta's murderer and
the blackmailer, telling it on the premise that they were the
same person. She said nothing about the most important
development. She'd decided not to tell Rumney; the imme-
diate motive for confiding in him would be that danger was
involved in delivering the ransom, but if there were danger to
Miss Pink because the kidnapping was genuine, then the
danger was as great for Caroline. Rumney would insist on
accompanying his guest, or he would tell the police; he
wouldn't stake one life against another, whereas she was
prepared to gamble. On the other hand, if—as had crossed
her mind fleetingly—there was a chance that Caroline had
turned on her father and was conspiring to rob him of fifty
thousand pounds, then Caroline's life was not in danger but
then neither was Miss Pink's (or so she argued). She confined
the kidnapping in a compartment of her mind and shut the
door on it, quickly, because if Wren killed Peta, he could kill

138

Caroline—and Miss Pink did not think that Caroline was involved in a conspiracy to rob her father.

Rumney was not surprised that Sarah was being blackmailed. The conversation at breakfast and Miss Pink's constraint at lunch-time had prepared him. What did astound him was Mossop's revelation to the man Cole that Peta had been stealing from the tills at Storms.

'But even that ties in,' he pointed out. 'Mossop was bound to find out, so she was murdered before she talked.'

'Mossop knew,' she corrected, 'unless he discovered why she was stealing money only after her death.'

A Land Rover came up the street and stopped outside the cow-house.

'That will be Arabella,' Rumney said. 'She went to town for some folk concert.'

The girl appeared at the half-door. 'The river's awfully high, Uncle Zeke; it's a good thing you moved those sheep from Quentin's land. I stopped in the Throat and it's almost up to the road.'

'You shouldn't stop in the Throat, girl; not after the rain we've had. There's always rocks coming down in the wet.'

'There are rocks on the road now; it's terrifying. But the rain's stopped.'

'For the moment; the forecast is more rain. Was the concert good?'

'Fabulous. Uncle Zeke, Jackson's van is in the big car park in Carnthorpe.'

'Is it?' Miss Pink exclaimed, her mind racing.

'Why, I didn't see you, Miss Pink; it's so dark. Yes, it's his van; I went over and looked.'

'Was there an attendant in the car park?'

'Not on a Sunday. I'm going in again tomorrow and I'll ask him when Jackson left it if you like, but it looks as if you're right; he's gone off with Caroline. I guess he'll hitch back from London, or wherever they went. It's starting to rain again; are you coming in for tea, Miss Pink?'

'I'm coming now.' She hesitated, then said casually, 'I'm going to see Harper this evening, Zeke, and then I may run into Carnthorpe to hear a lecture at the field society's place.'

'I don't know that that's wise; if there's a landslide in the Throat you may not be able to get back.'

'I'll manage somehow.'

In her room at Sandale House she stood at the window and thought about her position. A number of people held a piece of the puzzle and some, including Jackson Wren, held more than they'd divulged, or had been ascertained about them, but she alone held the bulk of it. But for the latest terrible development, it was now the time to go to the police; yet that was the last thing she could do. She knew all the arguments ranged against private negotiations with kidnappers but always one returned to the incontrovertible fact: that trying to trap the criminal endangered the life of his victim. Neither could she inform the police after she dropped the ransom money; it was essential to wait for Caroline's release. She knew that if it were her own daughter she would negotiate, so why should she put Harper's daughter in a lesser league?

There was a possibility that Caroline was already dead; that was a risk which had to be taken but—and here she was implacable—if she were dead, then the people responsible would be found. It crossed her mind that this sudden surge of ruthlessness was what the police felt when they were so adamantly opposed to private negotiation: justice not at all costs, but at cost. It was comparatively easy for the public to give the authorities moral support when a gang held hostages and made outrageous demands, but when the threat came home and you had talked to the victim on the other side of a fire two nights ago, and when you could see the light in the house of the second victim now, justice was nothing more than a word. She dropped the curtain and turned back to her room. The die cast, she was only a courier; there was nothing more that she could do. She was sorry for Harper; she was suddenly appalled to realise that she was far more sorry for him than she was for Caroline.

She went to Burblethwaite at seven o'clock. When she'd last seen him a few hours ago he'd been drained of vitality; now he looked like an old man. They sat over an electric heater and drank tea which she made, having brought milk across from the farm; he was beyond any domestic activity. What on earth could they talk about while they waited for the telephone call? Agonisingly, for her, he started to talk about Caroline and when she got over her initial shock she realised he was telling her what Caroline thought of New York, Tokyo, Cairo. He rambled on about the girl's friends among airline pilots and travelling executives. He was very proud of her social life. But at length his reminiscences ran out and he fell silent. Miss Pink tried to make conversation about the cottage, the dale, television. He wasn't listening. He asked, with a flicker of hope: 'How soon will they release her?'

She made an effort to be practical. 'The person who picks up the money will have to contact the one who's holding Caroline. If they communicate by phone, then she could call you as soon as she's free.'

'Yes.' He was expressionless. 'She'd do that.'

Fear held their minds and through the closed window they heard the sound of the flooded beck. Miss Pink hoped that there'd be no landslide in the Throat—for surely it was quite impossible that the drop would be in Sandale. That was too near home.

They talked desultorily of a dozen subjects, Miss Pink initiating them and words emerging from Harper's mouth like drips from a faulty tap until she asked suddenly: 'Why don't we start making a list of the numbers on those banknotes, then you can go to the police when Caroline's safe, and they can try to catch the gang by way of the money?'

'No.'

'Why not?'

His face flushed with anger. 'Because I say so.'

'It's hot money,' Miss Pink said.

The silence stretched. His face was no longer hopeless but hard and stubborn.

'Did you rob a bank?'

He looked at her without fear but with no sign of capitulation. 'It's money,' he said. 'It's the price of my girl's life.' She nodded agreement. 'I'll tell you something, miss.' He leaned forward. 'No one died for that money; you're not having to handle stuff with blood on it, don't worry.' He was bitter.

'I'm not thinking about myself. I was wondering if we could get some clue to the kidnapper by way of the money; obviously he knew you'd got it.'

'He didn't know. He guessed. The police are keeping an eye on me. Race tracks, you see; they watch everybody.'

'The local police?'

'Oh yes.'

'I see. So you think the information leaked down to Wren by way of the local bobby?'

'That looks like the score.' He'd sunk back into apathy. Suddenly the telephone rang, startling them. It was only seven-thirty. After the first shock Miss Pink thought that it was logical that the criminals wouldn't keep to schedule.

This time she didn't go to the phone but waited, concentrating her forces, trying to eliminate everything from her mind but the job in hand: to obey instructions and absorb every associated detail—like the timbre of a voice.

'He wants to speak to you.' Harper's voice was toneless. He was holding out the receiver. She stood up.

The instrument was slightly damp. 'Miss Pink here.'

'You've got the money?'

'Yes.'

'Go to Carnthorpe and take the road to the pass under Whirl Howe. Got that?'

'Yes.'

142

'Turn round at the car park at the top of the pass and come back the same way. At the second gate on the left, turn into the forestry and drive on the main track about half a mile —don't turn off nowhere—till you come to a shed in a big space. There's a row of fire beaters. Leave the money under the beaters, turn round and go home. Repeat that.'

She did so.

'You'll be under surveillance at intervals. If you see any cars, don't trouble remembering the number plates; they're false. And don't make a slip. Harper stays at home. Got that?'

'Yes.'

'You got your car with you now?'

'Yes.'

'Leave right away.' The line clicked and the dialling tone began.

'Give me a pencil,' Miss Pink said, holding a scratch pad and looking round.

'There's one by the directory. What did he say? Where are you going?'

She wrote down the instructions. 'I'm leaving this here. It's up to you to tell the police if anything goes wrong. If I can't get back for any reason then I'll ring you.' She wrote his number on the pad and tore off the page. 'Let's get the case in my car and I'll be off.'

She drove down the track and across the bridge. There were no lights anywhere except behind her in Burblethwaite; others were hidden by barns or thick curtains. She started down the lane, her windscreen wipers clacking busily.

As she drove she wondered where the waiting cars would be—or was that a blind? She thought that where this kind of activity was concerned, as few people as possible would be involved. The Lindbergh kidnapping had been the work of one man, and only two had been convicted in the McKay case. She remembered grimly that those victims had died. She was glad she hadn't asked the caller to furnish proof that

Caroline was still alive. Harper had only that hope to sustain him.

She passed the entrance to Storms' drive and changed down for the bend. Drops from the trees drummed on the roof. After High Hollins' gate there was water across the road and she took it carefully, praying.

For the next few hundred yards the road ran straight, with the meadows on the left which must be flooded; several inches had seeped through the wall to cover the tarmac. In her lights the long raised footway with its wooden railing gleamed wetly, then the rock wall of the Throat showed naked above the road and the tarmac was clear again.

The gorge was about a mile in length and the road curved tortuously. There were fallen stones on it, as Arabella had said, and as she came over incipient brows and the headlights dipped and swung on the right-hand bends, they showed her the river, seemingly on the same level as the highway, but it was no longer a river; it was a plunging mass of white water, shocking in its elemental power. You felt the very earth couldn't stand against it; that at any moment the whole gorge —crags, banks and hanging woods—would collapse like sand and slip into this tearing flood.

Suddenly she was calm. She changed gear carefully on the bends, never getting into top, not hearing the changes and the acceleration because the world held no other sound but the roar of water. And then she came to several big rocks in the road and could not pass. She stopped, put her handbrake on hard and, leaving the engine running, got out.

She had on an anorak but no waterproofs. She'd put up her hood but it was wrenched back immediately by the wind. Spray and rain came in waves and her spectacles streamed. There was one moment of stupefaction engendered by the noise and then she disregarded it, wiping her thumbs over her glasses to see her way to the rocks.

She had the pattern of them clear. If she moved one on the

144

left, the river side, she could squeeze past; if she cleared the way on the safer side, she had more work to do. The headlights shone on water, wet tarmac and the rock.

It was too big to lift. She bent and got both hands underneath. It rolled over and she followed, shuffling. The camber of the road favoured her. It rolled again and stopped. She wiped her glasses and paused, listening to other rolling sounds under the sound of water: it was boulders being battered down the river bed by the current.

She gave another heave, putting all her weight behind it, and the rock toppled over and vanished without splash or sound into the foam.

She sat in the car breathing hard and drying her spectacles on her handkerchief. Then she put the car in gear and, with her offside wheels grazing the remaining rocks, crept through the gap, her body pressed against her door in an ineffectual but instinctive cringe away from the deep.

At the end of the gorge there was more water across the road but then it took a slightly higher line and she had a clear run to Carnthorpe, passing the occasional light in cottage windows. It was curious to think of people sitting behind the curtains reading, sewing, watching television, knowing nothing of the bizarre business of the little car whose engine they heard going past their windows. But who did speculate on the horror that might exist on the other side of a glass screen?

Carnthorpe gleamed wet and empty and the lights served only to emphasise the abandonment of the streets to the rain. Somewhere at this moment the naturalists would be listening to the lichenologist. Somewhere Caroline was—waiting? Somewhere Caroline was. And somewhere: in a stationary car between street lights, in a dark yard, in the back of an empty car park, were eyes watching her pass? *How did they know her car?* Wren would have told them, she chided herself; she was fabricating bogies.

She took the road to the pass and after a mile or so of farmland and hardwoods, the ground started to rise and the forests began. Occasionally cars passed in the other direction, they and Miss Pink dipping their lights automatically. She felt a sense of comradeship with these unknown, unseen drivers who kept within the law, until she remembered that the criminals would dip their headlights too.

She did not know the Lakes well enough to identify the gateway as she approached from the bottom but there were very few, and about a mile from the top of the pass she started to look out for entrances, and when one appeared she tried to pierce the blackness outside her lights to discern a gleam of metal, but she saw no other car waiting, neither there, nor at the next entrance. Then she ran into cloud and dipped her lights. The gradient eased, she passed a big parking sign and put out her indicator.

At the top of the pass there were broad spaces on either side. She eased along, watching for the left-hand one. Here it was, the gravel entrance scarcely discernible against grass that was colourless in the mist-diffused light. She turned in but, not wanting to lose the way out again, went round on a hard lock and came back to the road immediately. If other cars were parked there, she couldn't see them; only the mist drifted through her beams.

She stopped momentarily and doused her lights to make sure nothing was coming, then she started back the way she had come.

She ran down the road carefully, watching for the first entrance. She passed it, came out of the cloud, realised it was dropping, and rolled on to the second gateway.

The forestry track was surfaced with chippings which were soft under her wheels. She hoped that she wouldn't get bogged down but reckoned that she was near enough to walk now. Half a mile, the voice on the telephone had said. She guessed that she was not alone in this section of the forest. Someone was listening to the sound of her engine; someone was waiting near the hut by the fire beaters. Now it showed in the lights: a small wooden bothy with a tin roof gleaming, and beside it: the rack of beaters. There was a turning circle and the track divided into three.

She turned and nosed back to the hut. She stopped the engine and got out.

The forest was alive with the soughing of the fir trees. The rain seemed less heavy than it had been at the lower altitude. She opened the rear door and dragged out the suitcase. She put it beside the beaters, returned to the car and drove back to the road.

There were lights coming up the hill from the direction of Carnthorpe. She was exhausted and hardly concentrating, except that she remembered to dip for the approaching traffic. She wondered how soon they would hear from Caroline.

Back in Burblethwaite they waited for the telephone to ring and talked as one does in bivouacs during a storm or waiting for the stretcher beside a corpse. Pondering the number of people who might have known that George Harper possessed money, if only temporarily, Miss Pink said: 'If anyone had suspicions about you, they'd have deepened when Caroline arrived. They didn't know she was your daughter presumably, and an expensive mistress implied that you were rich yourself.'

He nodded. 'I never meant her to come here. She turned up sudden like. You see, she doesn't know—' He looked away, his fingers plucking at the cover of his chair.

'She was too well-dressed,' Miss Pink mused.

'I took her to Paris when I was flush,' he recalled dreamily. 'It was a holiday for both of us. I gave her the Lotus too. I don't much care for money, myself, but I like to give Caroline things.'

She had no comment to make on this. After a while she

147

looked at her watch and remarked that she would have to go
to Sandale House or Rumney would start to worry. Harper,
who had been quiet for a while, agreed.

'You don't have to come back,' he told her.

'I'll come back; I'll bring a sleeping-bag. . . .'

'Then you'd have to tell Rumney.'

'I would tell him *where* I am; I don't have to tell him why.'

In the circumstances the last part of this was untrue but
they both knew it would be unbearable for him to wait on his
own for a telephone call which might not come. She looked
at him thoughtfully, trying to think of a good reason to give
to Rumney for spending the night at Burblethwaite and at
that point there was a knock on the door. Harper's drawn
face, for one moment, was suffused with joy, until he realised
that Caroline wouldn't knock.

'You answer it,' he said.

It was Rumney. He looked worried and sounded jolly and
artificial. 'Heard you come back some time ago,' he said,
peering past her at Harper, then walking in without invitation.
' 'Evening, George. . . .' He looked closely at the other man.
'Something's wrong.'

Miss Pink stood there in consternation. All Harper's
suffering was in his eyes and now he dropped his head in his
hands and groaned. Rumney looked from Miss Pink to the
door, shocked, and torn between his indelicacy at witnessing
another man's collapse and the need to share Miss Pink's
responsibility with her. She was looking at the telephone.

'Can I do anything?' he asked.

'It's George's problem,' she said meaningly.

'It doesn't matter now,' Harper said.

'It's not been very long,' she reminded him. 'it's not two
hours yet.'

'He's had time to ring the others; he's passed a dozen
kiosks by now.'

'Consideration for people's feelings isn't one of their finer points,' Miss Pink said, and cursed herself for the pomposity.

Rumney shifted his feet and she motioned to a chair. He sat down quietly, watching Harper.

'She won't come back,' Harper said.

'No!' It was wrenched from her, and then she realised it could be taken for agreement. 'Perhaps the fellow they sent hasn't found the right place; he could have got lost in the forest.' Harper said nothing. 'Tell Zeke,' she pleaded.

'You tell him.'

So she told him. It didn't take long; the facts were simple and sparse. All the horror had been in the waiting—since one o'clock yesterday afternoon for Harper. When she finished, with the information that they were now waiting for the telephone to ring, Rumney was harrowed and speechless. At length he suggested that she return to Sandale House while he spent the night at Burblethwaite. She could tell his mother merely that he was keeping Harper company. 'Mother won't question it,' he assured her.

Eventually she said goodnight to Harper and went out. It was raining. Rumney came with her to the car and sat in the passenger's seat.

'Don't leave him for long,' she urged.

'I'm just going back. Do you think she's alive?'

'God knows ... and her abductor.'

'When do we give up hoping and tell the police?'

'This is the worst moment of all,' she admitted. 'At least, before, we were in the hands of the kidnapper, doing what he told us to do. Now we don't know whether we're on our own or not. If we knew she was dead we should tell them immediately; there's no doubt about that. But if she's alive, could telling them jeopardise her safety? Suppose for some reason they're still holding her, suppose the man who was meant to pick up the money has had an accident: is in hospital or even dead? If we told the police, and the search started for Wren tonight, it could be on the radio tomorrow morning, and then

149

they might kill her. In any case,' she added angrily, 'what do we lose by not telling them? The gang gets away, that's all: better a number of guilty men escape than an innocent person dies—isn't that the foundation of British justice?' She was bitter. 'I'm not telling them tonight. You won't either, not after an hour with Harper.'

Chapter 14

MISS PINK WOKE to knocking, a flood of light, and
Arabella standing against the sunshine, her dark little face
harassed, a cup of tea in her hand. 'Zeke told me,' she said.
'No one's phoned; no one at all. What are we going to do?
Oh, God, what a way to wake anyone!'

'No harm done.' Miss Pink was equable, sipping her tea
and getting the feel of the day. A robin was singing above the
noise of the beck.

'That poor man,' Arabella said. 'I can't believe it's happened. I suppose it's true—Caroline couldn't be playing some
ghastly trick?'

Miss Pink thought of Peta's murder and the blackmail.
'No,' she said, and knew it was the end of that possibility.
'It's true.'

'Where do you think she—? Where would they take her?'

'The police will look for her car.'

'Zeke brought George over for breakfast. That man didn't
eat yesterday!'

'I know; I couldn't get him to eat.'

Harper, seated at the breakfast table, was, as she'd expected
to find him; dull, shocked, hopeless: an automaton eating
what was put before him and saying nothing. Rumney took
her aside and said that he'd sent for the doctor. 'He didn't
sleep all night,' he told her, indicating Harper. 'Quentin will
give him a sedative, I expect; he can sleep in my room.'

'Someone ought to be at Burblethwaite in case the phone
rings.'

'Lucy Fell's over there; she'll ring us immediately if anything happens. She had to be told, you know.'

151

'Yes; everyone will know in an hour or two. I must go to Carnthorpe and see the police.'

He nodded. 'We can't do anything, and they've got the manpower; she could be anywhere between here and London.'

Arabella went to Carnthorpe too, taking the Rumney Land Rover. They went separately because Miss Pink didn't know how long she would be kept at the police station. Before they left she said to the girl, out of Harper's hearing, 'You might get into conversation with that car-park attendant; it would have been quite early Saturday morning that Wren left his van: before ten.'

Workmen were clearing the road in the Throat. The water level was still very high and the torrent even more terrifying seen in daylight, but everything sparkled and there were rainbows in the spray. Miss Pink felt the sighs of delayed shock rising to the surface and suppressed them ruthlessly.

The C.I.D. man was a chief inspector called Hendry. There were no recriminations; there might be later but now a machine started to roll and the machine demanded facts. Miss Pink supplied them. There was a small exchange when Hendry told her that they'd been keeping an eye on Harper not as a professional punter but as a London villain. This was no more than she'd suspected but she was aware of an element of surprise on the part of Hendry when she told him that Harper had kept fifty thousand pounds in Burblethwaite. 'But he was only a labourer!' he remarked, and asked her what the notes looked like.

She had wondered if they might be able to concentrate on the kidnapping to the exclusion of the blackmailing letters (thinking of Sarah Noble and the dead hiker) but there was no chance. Question led to question, explanation to explanation, and at last it seemed that everything was revealed, everything that she knew, even to the theft of Rumney's sheep. And if she was aware of disapproval lurking in the background she had a momentary sense of balance redressed when she told them about the priest.

'Blood on it?' Hendry repeated. He was new to his rank: young, alert, never missing a nuance or moment of hesitation. He was going bald quickly but he still had the hard heavy body of a rugby player. He had sharp blue eyes and a thin mouth.

'I thought it was blood,' she admitted.

'But you didn't do anything about it.'

'It could have been salmon blood.'

His mouth thinned further in a closed smile. She was not intimidated; she didn't think that the police would have found Caroline if she had told them yesterday morning that the priest had blood on it. Hendry thought that here was a woman who knew herself morally in the right and, recognising that her—to him—irresponsible behaviour was in the past, he accepted it without approving it, and concentrated on the present. He said that he was going up to Sandale and asked her to return there herself.

Arabella followed her up to her room. Harper was sedated, she said, and Quentin wouldn't allow him to be interviewed for another half hour. The police were at Burblethwaite, having released Lucy Fell from a useless vigil. There were more police at Coneygarth and she guessed some were with Lucy at Thornbarrow. 'And probably everyone down the road is being questioned,' she said grimly. 'I know it's terrible, Miss Pink, especially when you think of Sarah, but I've got this awful smug feeling: thank God we've done nothing wrong! How selfish can you get?'

'Perfectly natural,' Miss Pink observed. 'Did you learn anything in Carnthorpe about Saturday?'

'I found out quite a bit but I don't see how it helps. They arrived in the two cars some time before ten o'clock, the attendant said. Jackson was in climbing gear and wearing shades; Caroline attracted his attention—her car is so distinctive for these parts. They left both cars and were away for only a short time. Caroline bought a pair of sneakers.'

'What!'

'You know: canvas boots, for climbing.'

'How do you know that?'

'If they were away for so short a time, it was likely they'd bought something, besides, the attendant said she'd been carrying a small parcel when they came back. I thought of presents and I tried the crafts shops first and then I thought it was odd for Jackson to wear breeches to drive to London for a weekend and I remembered about their making arrangements to climb but one can't climb without boots, so I tried the climbing shop. That was it; she'd bought sneakers. I saw the guy who served them but he's new there and he didn't know Jackson so they didn't chat. He remembered Caroline of course.'

Miss Pink was silent and after a while Arabella went on: 'They left in Caroline's car but the attendant didn't see which way they went; he couldn't because of the houses.'

'Someone may have seen them; the police will find out which way they went.'

'It was on the radio news; they're looking for the Lotus.'

'You could hide a hundred cars in the forests under Whirl Howe,' Miss Pink said absently.

'But there aren't any crags round there.' They stared at each other. 'I did a lot of climbing with Jackson,' Arabella explained, and looked puzzled. 'Why couldn't they have had a climbing accident?'

'That doesn't explain the kidnappers' threats and the ransom demand.'

'Oh no. I was clutching at straws.' Her little face puckered again. 'But if they went climbing—I mean, don't the sneakers imply climbing?—how does that tie in with her being kidnapped?'

Miss Pink said slowly: 'He told her that they would climb in order to get her to some . . . hut? Cottage? Are there any

154

crags above buildings: a closed building where you could confine a person? It would have to be a remote crag.'

Arabella sat on the bed and pressed her fingers to her forehead. 'There's a climbing hut round the other side of Helvellyn: Rushwaite Lodge?'

'A climbing hut's no good because of the likelihood of the owners turning up, particularly at a weekend. It's Ruthwaite Lodge, not Rushwaite: up above Greenside lead mines . . . no, they're in the next valley—'

'Mines!'

'Mines?'

'Mine buildings. Some of them are in good condition and if she were tied up it wouldn't matter if he couldn't lock her in; in fact—' Arabella shuddered, 'it wouldn't be necessary to put her in a building if she were bound and gagged.'

'She'd die if she were in the open; remember the weather.'

'Well. . . . But I didn't mean the open air. What about a cave? Why—' She stopped and stared at the other. 'Wasn't it raining on Saturday? Of course it was! It poured.'

'Quite late, surely?'

'The cloud was low at daybreak—so that rules out a high crag to start with; Jackson hated greasy rock. I'm sure all the rock would have been greasy, even at a low altitude. It did rain early, Miss Pink, because I did some washing and had to hang it in the barn, then Grannie and I had coffee. I guess it was raining at eleven. I know where they'd go! The Rat Hole in Borrowdale! That's where everyone goes on a wet day.'

'But if everyone goes there—'

'Oh yes, there are crowds, particularly on a Saturday.'

'—he wouldn't go there, would he?'

There was silence broken by Arabella in a small voice.

'Miss Pink.'

'Yes?'

'There's Shivery Knott.'

'Zeke said there were caves,' Miss Pink said quietly, 'I came

155

back under Shivery Knott on Saturday afternoon and there was something in the woods.'

Chief Inspector Hendry was talking to the doctor in the living room and two strange men stood by the window. Hendry turned as Miss Pink came downstairs and entered the room. She nodded to Quentin Bright and she told them about Shivery Knott. Hendry looked doubtful and, indeed, the chain of reasoning by which she and Arabella had arrived at this point seemed flimsy in the telling.

'Where would they leave the car?' Hendry asked.

It was Bright who answered. 'They'd go up to the scenic car park above the Throat: you know the one, where the car rolled over before the wardens put the tree trunks along the edge. There's a path going along past Mart Howe to the top of Shivery Knott. Of course, the quickest way to the crag is from here, but since the car isn't here . . .'

'I'll send a couple of men up there,' Hendry said.

'But he'd have moved the car,' Miss Pink pointed out.

Hendry's eyes narrowed. 'Are you suggesting that he's holding her in a cave at this place?'

She restrained a sigh. Quentin Bright said: 'It goes in for some distance; climbers leave it alone because, if you want to explore a cave system, there's a far better one in Borrowdale. I don't think anyone goes to Shivery Knott nowadays. We've been there because we're residents and we're climbers and we go there once out of curiosity, that's all.'

'Climbers leave it alone,' Hendry repeated. 'Do you have to be a climber to get inside?'

'You need a rope,' Bright said. 'A layman couldn't do it on his own.'

'I've got no men to spare; even if I had a climber on the strength, which I haven't.' Hendry looked at Miss Pink.

'I'll go,' she said, thinking it was a cue.

'Are you leaving immediately?' Bright asked. 'I'd like to

156

come with you, but Hendry's going to see Harper and I ought to be present; he's not in good shape.'

'Now, Doctor, you said he can take it; he's got to take it in the circumstances. Rumney might go with Miss Pink.'

'How long will you be with Harper?'

Hendry spread his hands and the doctor turned back to Miss Pink. 'I'll come up to the crag afterwards, if you haven't returned.'

The sun had gone behind a bank of cloud when they left the hamlet and took the path past Coneygarth. The front door of the cottage was open but the opening looked sinister rather than welcoming.

'More rain coming,' Rumney said gloomily. He was wearing old climbing boots and a stained anorak, and he carried a rope.

'Does Shivery Knott flood?'

'I wouldn't think so. The system's on the slant, d'you see; the water can't lie in there.'

They left the packhorse track and struck up through the trees. There was no path but here and there the undergrowth looked as if it had been flattened although that could have been the result of the torrential rain. No marks showed in the pockets of washed soil between the scree.

They came to the foot of the crag which was really nothing more than a pile of gigantic blocks separated by cracks and chimneys. The entrance to the system was by way of a chasm where the walls converged to a roof above their heads, and at the end they climbed up broken steps to an enclosed space where they had to start using their headlamps. They didn't put the rope on. Rumney had brought it for emergencies. He told her that he had been through the system once, looking for a dog, and he'd had no difficulty unroped and alone.

They left the enclosed space by crawling through a slit at floor level. This was horizontal for a few yards and then it widened so that one could stand. Miss Pink felt her age. The

157

strenuous activity was tiring her and she thought how ridiculous it was to imagine that Jackson Wren could have brought Caroline here. Caroline demanded romance and heroic exploits but in this place the most virile man must lose his dignity. When she joined Rumney, after twenty feet or so of the most racking contortions, for the underground crack was narrow and the walls held her like a vice as she tried to force her way upwards, she suggested they retreat.

'Not likely,' Rumney said stoutly. 'With our figures we could get stuck in that crack.'

'But there's no one here. They would have heard us by now, and shouted.'

'Gagged?' he suggested. 'Forced to keep silent?'

'What! You think Wren's here as well?'

'No, there's no one here.' He was reassuring. 'But we're not going back. I certainly didn't when I was looking for that dog. I went on, and there's a way out somewhere. Are you ready?'

Their torch beams showed a broken cavern; they were in the bowels of the crag. Beyond Rumney was what appeared to be a bottomless hole but as he climbed down and she shone her torch beyond and below him she could see ledges and bulging walls and he was descending easily, telling her where the holds were. She played the light on the ground at her feet, thinking that she should have done this before, looking for traces of other people. There was nothing but the bedrock, and small stones in the crevices.

'You can follow now,' he called from the depths.

She lowered herself over the edge, concentrating on the mental pattern of pockets and ledges which she'd seen from the top. Rumney was standing on a wide ledge above another big drop partly choked with fallen blocks. At its right-hand end it must be very deep or very long or both; the torches couldn't penetrate the darkness. Leftwards the ledge ran into a slab which sloped steeply down to a glimmer of daylight.

158

'That must be the other entrance,' he said with satisfaction. 'Let's see.'

They descended the slab which was about thirty feet high and scored with horizontal cracks, the lower section pallid in the natural light. They stepped off the bottom and walked through another chasm to the open air; they were halfway up the crag and a broken gully dropped to the scree at an easy angle.

'Is that all of it?' she asked.

'There's that space at the top of the slab: the chasm with the big blocks.'

'I suppose we'd better—?' She was cross with herself for having suggested this silly caper. 'We ought to be able to tell Hendry we've examined the whole system.'

They turned and climbed the slab, then moved along the ledge to a point where they could step down on to the tumbled blocks. 'Watch these,' she warned, 'they're none too stable.' A big one rocked under her feet with a muffled crack of stone on stone.

They descended carefully, kicking each block before trusting their weight on it. They reached the bed of the chasm, or so they thought. Rumney directed his torch to the left where the ground slanted down between great red walls that gleamed wet in the light. At the end was a tall and tapering slit, too narrow for the passage of anything fatter than a fox. Cold air came through it. Miss Pink shone her torch rightwards.

'What on earth—? It's a rope!'

'That's not rope.' They moved forward. It *was* rope: dark in colour, and it was strained horizontally across the rock.

'Mind,' he warned, 'there's a great hole here: a chasm on a lower level.'

'Here's a peg,' Miss Pink said.

The rock receded inwards to form a large oval hollow, the walls of which were coated with some deposit that sparkled silver in their lights. An alloy peg had been driven into a crack and from it the rope ran taut across the ledge and disappeared. It was under tremendous strain and immovable.

They felt their way carefully to the edge of the pit. They didn't see the bottom, not because it was invisible but because their lights were arrested by what was on the end of the rope. Caroline was found.

They moved back to the recess.

'We can't tell it's her,' Miss Pink said sadly.

'It's like her hair—reddish.'

'Can we get down?'

'We'd better see if we can.'

'Give me the rope; I'll uncoil it.'

'Of course we can get down!' he exclaimed. 'It's a matter of getting back.' He moved away from her, prospecting along the ledge.

'We can climb down easily,' he called back, 'and up again. We don't really need the rope.'

'We ought to get close to her: to identify her. There's Harper, you see; there should be no doubt.'

'I'd forgotten Harper.'

Miss Pink fastened the middle of the rope to the peg. 'Will it reach the bottom?' she asked. 'It can't be sixty feet.' The rope was a hundred and twenty feet long. She coiled it and, stepping to the edge, threw the coils expertly into the abyss. They heard the dry rattle as the rope settled on the ground.

'By the sound of that, it's only about twenty feet,' she observed. 'I'll make sure it hasn't snagged.'

She peered over. The doubled rope descended straight and even beside the body. She glanced at the slack on the floor of the chasm, went to turn away, then checked.

'That's odd.'

'What is?'

'Come here. What's that in the bottom?'

'Why, it looks like— It is! What—?' He turned to her. 'Could that be Wren?'

They stared at the second body and now they could make out the twisted legs, a hand—but no face.

160

'What an incredible accident,' he breathed, 'both of them!'

She passed the rope round herself. Rumney directed the beam of his torch on the anchorage. She walked backwards to the edge, the rope tight to the peg. She teetered for a moment, spreading her feet, getting her weight balanced, then she started walking down the wall, leaning out on the rope which, round one thigh and the opposite shoulder, ran out slowly as she descended.

She came to the body which hung heavily against the rock but moved when she touched it. She drew level with the face, held herself in position with one hand and lifted the chestnut hair. The wide eyes of Caroline stared back at her.

There was a lot of rope festooned about the body, and a loop round the neck. It was from the neck that the rope ran taut to the peg above. The girl's arms were strained backwards, the hands behind her. Miss Pink felt down the arms to the cold wrists. They were tightly bound together by something which felt like hemp line. The fingers were quite limp.

There was also a rope round the waist but this descended to the chasm as did another emerging from the looped confusion about the body. Miss Pink moved lower. Caroline was wearing dark slacks and bright blue canvas boots. The ankles were also bound with hemp. She got one arm behind the straight legs and lifted. The knees bent easily.

'Well?' Rumney's voice came from above.

'It's her; she must have hanged. The rope's round the neck. She's been here a long time.'

'Why?'

'Stone-cold and no *rigor;* it passes off in two days.'

'But that takes us back to Saturday afternoon!'

'I'll go on; I'm not very comfortable here.'

She continued to the ground while Rumney climbed down the rocks at the side. She regarded the other body which lay as it had fallen, with twisted limbs. It was Wren. His head was slightly to one side so that the right profile was exposed and about one inch above the eyebrow was a small circular wound which had bled. Rumney approached.

'It's him,' she said, 'I think he's been shot.'

'*Shot?* You mean it isn't an accident?' He stooped and shone his torch on the head. 'You're right. Killed himself, d'you think—after Caroline died?'

'Her ankles and wrists are tied with hemp line.'

'Good God!'

'Let's see if we can find a gun.'

It was quite close to the body: a Walther PPK ·22, fallen between two rocks which was why they hadn't seen the metal gleam.

'There will be fingerprints on that jacket,' Miss Pink said. 'We'll leave it for Hendry. I wonder where it came from? How are the police going to get here, and all the forensic people?'

'That's their problem; they'll probably get the Mountain Rescue chaps to lower—'

'Listen!' Above their heads a rock had moved. 'Put your torch out,' she hissed.

They stood in the dark, listening, staring upwards. There was not so much as a pin-point of light. Miss Pink knew the meaning of pitch black. Then slowly, as her eyes became accustomed to the totality of this new sensation she realised that it wasn't total; at some point way up and out to the right, there was movement. It grew and became a glow which increased until it stretched their nerves to snapping point and the rock walls of these modest caves loomed and bulged with an illusion of bulk that rivalled a great show-cavern. Then, in the centre of the glow a bright speck appeared like an anti-climax, vanished and reappeared as someone swung a torch.

'Zeke!' It was a shriek. 'Rumney!' That was better; they breathed again.

'We're down here, Quentin,' Rumney called. 'But watch out: there's an enormous chasm at the end of the ledge.'

'Where? Oh, I see; what are you doing down there? Found anything?'

162

'Indeed we have: both of them.'

'Well? In what shape?'

'They're both dead.'

'Good Lord!' There was a pause while he digested this. 'Can I get down?'

Rumney showed him the easy descent and he joined them at the bottom, talking quietly and intimately now that they were all together. They directed their torches on the suspended body and Miss Pink gave him the details.

'Tied?' he repeated. 'Tied and hanged? Unbelievable!'

'And Wren's been shot,' Rumney said.

The doctor stooped and peered at the wound. He held the wrist and raised it gently; it was quite limp.

'I've got no thermometer,' he muttered. 'I didn't expect to find this. But *rigor's* passed off; I'd say he's been here the better part of two days. Is the girl stiff?'

'She's quite limp,' Miss Pink said.

'Tied up by Wren?' The doctor was questioning himself. 'And then he went away and came back to find her dead— and shot himself? Where's the gun?'

They showed him the Walther. 'I wonder where that came from?' he mused. 'It's not the kind of thing I associate with Wren.' Then, briskly: 'We must get back to Hendry—and there's Harper. I was there when they questioned him. I think he's halfway prepared for this.'

'Really?' Miss Pink said drily, but they didn't hear; they were already on their way to the outside world.

It seemed to her that they had been underground for hours, and to be in daylight again was a blessed relief. The cloud had dropped and there was moisture in the air, but the open country, the gnarled oaks, grass, Sandale's hamlet clustering round the packhorse bridge, all these were homely and familiar after the starkness of those awful rock walls impending in the light of their lamps.

They slithered down the gully and stopped at the foot of the crag. The splash of the waterfall came to them and Miss

Pink said calmly: 'I heard him: at four o'clock on Saturday afternoon. There was someone blundering about just at this spot. I was on the packhorse track and it was nearly dark. Perhaps he'd just found her.'

'But surely,' the doctor said, 'he'd have killed himself when he found her, not gone away and come back?'

'He had to go down to Coneygarth for the gun,' Rumney put in.

The doctor turned to him. 'Then he'd have shot himself in Coneygarth surely? You don't pick up a gun, determined to kill yourself, and climb back through this wood and enter the caves and go up that slab and along the ledge to kill yourself at a certain spot. It's too devious.'

'That's irrelevant,' Miss Pink said.

The men were astonished. 'Irrelevant?' Rumney exclaimed.

'Because if he died on Saturday, who did I speak to last night? Who told me where to take the money?'

Chapter 15

S HE DID NOT return to the hamlet with them but
made no secret of her intentions: she would walk to the scenic
car park beyond Mart Howe, the place where Caroline's car
might be. Rumney objected but she pointed out that he and
the doctor could come back to the crag with the police; she
wasn't needed. 'Besides,' she added, 'I want to think, and
Hendry's questions at the moment would only muddle me. It's
a peculiar situation.' As she said it, she realised that this was
a considerable understatement.

They couldn't detain or dissuade her and they parted, Miss
Pink scrambling up the side of the crag to a small cairn that
marked its summit. From here a narrow path ran off in a
north-easterly direction through heather and scrub, rising
gently towards a crest of grey rocks which must be Mart
Howe.

She walked quickly, skirting the rocky knoll and coming, in
about twenty minutes, to a fringe of woodland. The path led
her through silver birches and the ubiquitous oaks to a clearing on the lip of an escarpment. Tree trunks had been placed
in position along the edge and below her the main valley was
revealed with its lake grey and tranquil under the cloud ceiling. It was a magnificent view-point but she wasn't interested
in scenery. There had been prints of gumboots on the path,
going towards Shivery Knott, but only in the one direction,
and she wasn't surprised to find Cole's Aston Martin in the
otherwise empty car park. She wondered how she'd missed
him.

For a while she roamed about the woods, but with the
leaves stripped from the trees she could see for a considerable
distance, and if Caroline's Lotus had been concealed here,

165

there was no trace of it now, and the rain had washed out any tyre tracks. She came back to the car park and tried the doors of the Aston Martin. They were locked. She started home by the way she had come.

As she approached Mart Howe she saw a figure ahead and mentally prepared herself, recognising the perky walk, the olive green cagoule of Daniel Cole. As they drew nearer she had the feeling that he too was prepared, but then any walkers, approaching over a distance in lonely country, have an air of self-consciousness.

Cole had a pair of binoculars slung round his neck. They greeted each other with studied casualness and he evinced no surprise to find her in this place. His eyes were hard and she noticed again how aquiline his features were, not in the least blurred by good living. At a tangent, her mind worried at his origins. Suddenly she realised that they were both waiting: herself for his questions—and he? For her explanation of her presence here? She had a most unusual feeling of intimidation and she was uneasy.

'How did he die?' Cole asked.

'Who?' She fought for time, her face blank.

'Wren.'

'I don't know what you're talking about.'

'You found Wren inside that cliff.' He gestured impatiently. 'I saw you come out and I heard what you said.'

'What did I say?'

'You said, "If he died on Saturday, who did I speak to last night? Who told me where to leave the money?"'

'I have to go down, Mr Cole; the police are waiting.'

'Rumney and Bright will have told the police. I'm the Press.'

'That's exactly why I'm going down. You came here because of Peta Mossop's murder; your assignment has nothing to do with conservation.' He said nothing, watching her. 'The police will issue a statement,' she said.

166

'I doubt it. I went a little way inside myself, but I haven't got a torch with me. It looks a dangerous place. Do you think the police will want sightseers up here? They're not going to tell the Press until they get the body out, perhaps not then.'

'So you're going to phone your paper with an exclusive story.'

'No.' A pause. 'Not yet. Not if you tell me what you found. You have to tell me, you know.' She showed her astonishment. 'Look,' he pressed, 'you can't stop me going back to my car now, any more than I can stop you returning to Sandale. But if I go down to the valley, the first thing I'm going to do will be to find a telephone and release what I know: that Wren's been found dead in a cave. Within an hour the reporters will be here in hordes, and then the public.'

'That's blackmail,' Miss Pink said.

'So how did he die?'

'You said if I told you, you wouldn't release it. Why not?'

'Because, like you, I want to know who telephoned you and made demands for money.'

'How do you know even that?'

'You said so: outside the cave; voices carry. I saw the doctor go inside and I hung about, and then you all came out. I was behind a rock near the bottom so I only heard the last bit of your conversation.'

'Why were you up here in the first place?'

'Two things. Mossop told me about these caves and I've been watching all the police activity. I even photographed the packhorse bridge and realised my presence wasn't exactly welcome. In fact, next time I show my nose in Sandale I wouldn't be surprised if I'm asked some questions. I saw you and Rumney leave the hamlet—and I've got field glasses. Mossop told me where you'd be bound for and how I could get there easily without following you. And although the police have been to the hotel they weren't there when I rang Mossop, so he was able to tell me they were looking for this girl and her car. It didn't take long to put two and two together. I'm not a bad reporter.'

'I can believe that,' she said drily.

'How did Wren die?'

'There's a wound in his head and a gun close by.'

'What kind of gun?'

'A Walther PPK ·22.'

His eyes glazed. After a moment he asked softly: 'And was there any sign of the girl?'

She looked away. When he spoke again his tone was flat. 'The girl was there.'

'Yes.'

'How did she die, Miss Pink?'

She told him. His eyes bored into hers. He asked questions. It was a difficult situation to explain to a non-climber and one who had never been inside a cave system, but he was intelligent. He asked how she thought it had happened.

'I can't speculate; you'll have to ask the police.'

'You'll know better than them; it's a specialist's job. You must have some idea.'

'The first reaction is that she was hanged by accident, and that he committed suicide when he found her.'

'But you don't believe that.' She blinked, against her will implying confirmation. 'Why not?' he asked.

Her shoulders slumped. 'He wasn't the type.'

'But you think the girl fell over by accident?'

She asked mildly: 'Who shot Wren?'

'Yes,' he said thoughtfully, 'who else is in it? Where did you drop the money?'

So he knew about that too. She told him where, watching his face and learning nothing.

'Did you see any vehicles in the forest?'

'No.'

'None on the road?'

'Some came up the hill as I left the forest; I took no notice

168

of them. How did you know about the kidnapping, Mr Cole?'

'I told you: Mossop and deduction for most of it; you're telling me the rest.'

It could be true—and he had heard what she said at the foot of the crag.

'Now what will you do?' she asked.

'I'm going to Sandale. I have to see the police. I suspect they'll put an embargo on any Press release and I'll have to go along with that, but I've got most of it already; I'm streets ahead of the competition once they give me the green light.'

'I think you could be of assistance, Mr Cole.'

'Oh? How?'

'We might work together,' she said carefully.

'What's your interest, dear?'

'I liked Caroline. I need to find the person behind Wren.'

' "Need"?'

'Yes.'

They studied each other. 'Strange as it may seem,' he said, 'I have values too. I don't like kidnappers and I detest blackmailers. No—' as she made a movement of impatience, '—you know what I'm referring to. Certainly I forced you to tell me the story but I didn't extort money from you; I didn't make your life hell.' He said it balefully and saw she was surprised. 'Perhaps I've met more blackmailers than you have.' He smiled, but not with his eyes.

'Where were you at seven-thirty last night, Mr Cole?'

'I was in Mossop's bar.'

'Was anyone else there?'

'Mossop, of course.' He thought for a moment. 'The fellow who waited on me at dinner looked in. There must have been a cook in the kitchen—a woman, that's right; she came in the back and Mossop gave her a Guinness. Why?'

'The kidnapper rang me at seven-thirty.'

'So you're considering me in the role. And Wren was shot

169

on Saturday. I lunched in London with friends on Saturday and I left to come up here about four o'clock. I think I arrived at the hotel at nine. And then I was talking to Mossop—after the customers had gone—until late that night.'

Miss Pink said: 'I don't think you need the money. You have all the signs of affluence; you seem to be a satisfied person—and sane; you'd never hang around afterwards when things have gone wrong—'

'They needn't have gone wrong, dear; presumably the killer got his money.'

'But two people have died!'

He shrugged. 'I suppose he meant originally to keep Caroline alive or she would have been killed once they reached the cave and there would have been no need to tie her hands and feet. Did he intend to kill Wren or was that a contingency plan?' He considered this while Miss Pink stared at him in astonishment. 'Oh, yes.' He acknowledged her consternation. 'They don't have any regard for life, these people, and less for suffering: look at that poor beggar, Harper. The girl died through an accident but after that Wren would have cracked, so he had to be killed. That was a mistake. The police might have believed it to be suicide, but then the kidnapper went ahead with the plan to get the money. Without the telephone calls the police might think only Wren had been in it, but with him dead and the money gone—'

'That's circumstantial,' she argued. 'It's depending on Wren dying on Saturday. They might not be able to prove when he died, so he could have made the last call at seven-thirty yesterday. As for the money, again it's dependent on time of death. He could have picked it up, in which case, where is it now? Alternatively it could have been removed by someone unconnected with the crime: poachers, a courting couple, anyone who happened to be in the forest last evening.'

'Very far-fetched,' Cole said pleasantly. 'You're looking at it from the policeman's point of view. Let's be realistic. Your kidnapper is a person who needs money—or someone who's keeping up pretences—'

'Actually,' she said, 'we were thinking in those terms for—'

'For the blackmailer,' he completed, 'and the person who killed Peta. Mossop's been talking—and other people.'

'Wren fitted the bill for the greedy, impoverished type, but he hadn't the intelligence for blackmail, least of all for this: the kidnapping.'

'Someone used him.'

They exchanged glances without subterfuge. 'You know them all,' he reminded her. 'Run through them.'

'What, now?' She was exhausted after the caves and the discovery of the bodies. She craved a cup of tea.

'You did say I could be of assistance.'

She shifted her feet. 'The doctor's wife,' she said petulantly. 'This is silly.'

He ignored the last part. 'I met her.' She raised her eyebrows. How he had got about! 'I have migraine,' he explained. 'I called at the surgery for some tablets and met both of them. Nice people.'

'Sarah Noble.'

'She was being blackmailed. And such an old dear. Not Sarah.'

'Her husband,' she said weakly.

'I met him at the Brights'. He's not a killer; the type who might strangle his mistress in a rage, but not a plotter. He could have killed Peta, but he's not responsible for this business—' He gestured towards Shivery Knott. 'He hasn't the guts for a kidnapping.'

'There's Mossop.'

'The same applies: a petty criminal only.'

'That's quite definite?'

'Receiving stolen goods,' he said lightly, 'and stealing Rumney's sheep: that's Mossop's level of crime. And—' He stopped and his eyes shifted.

'And what?'

'—moving Peta's body from his premises because he was terrified of being suspected of murder. An immoral little runt: more concerned with carrying on his fringe activities than in finding his wife's killer.'

'You make him sound the sadistic type who could have been the kidnapper all the same.'

'No, he's terrified out of his wits. Kidnappers are cool.'

'This one may not be. We don't know.'

Cole stared at her. 'Who's cracking in Sandale?'

'Mossop.'

'No, dear; he'd have cracked by now. I've had him drunk.'

'I see.'

He returned to a mental list and she realised how much work he must have put in since his arrival and what a formidable memory he had. 'Then we come to the hamlet. Harper and Wren are out of the running. That leaves Rumney.'

'No.'

'Well, where was he at the relevant times?'

'But it's not logical; he asked me to come here to try to help him. He was appalled at Peta's death—'

'Who wasn't? And he discovered all the bodies. Where was he, dear?'

'There are so many times concerned.'

'Your telephone call yesterday at seven-thirty. Where was he then?'

'I presume: at Sandale House.'

'Who else was there?'

'His old mother and his niece.'

'That enchanting American child? I met her.'

'Harper had the first call at one o'clock on Saturday,' she went on. 'The others were yesterday: at midday, at one o'clock and at seven-thirty.'

'I'd like to know more about Rumney's movements.'

'You're quite wrong,' she said firmly. 'And then there's

Lucy Fell. We were looking for someone poor. Rumney and Lucy are rich people.'

He was preoccupied. 'People who look like farm labourers usually are. Labourers look like stockbrokers. That was a nice piece of tweed though—forty years ago. His jacket, I mean: the one without any buttons.'

'That's all of them,' she said impatiently. The craving for tea was back. 'And don't forget the kidnapper must have killed Peta as well. There can't be two murderers in the dale.'

'Where was Lucy when Peta was killed?'

She stared, and then decided to humour him. 'It was a Friday. Denis Noble dined with her at Thornbarrow and stayed the night there. And Lucy's ruled out—'

'Yes, dear?'

'Well, I suppose you know almost everything now. Lucy was a victim too; she wasn't being blackmailed, but she had an abusive letter.'

'Really? I noticed an odd reaction when I suggested yesterday that I might find a skeleton in her bread cupboard. What was her secret?'

'Oh, it was fabricated—and Lucy didn't keep it a secret; she told me without my prompting. Her letter accused her of burying a baby in her own garden. Why—' she'd caught his expression, 'you don't believe it?'

'Of course not; it's just what you'd expect. All anonymous letters relate to the victim's activities. Poor little Peta asking for trouble because she's a nympho—and getting it; Sarah loses control when she drinks; Mossop is a cinch for a neighbour with a suspicious mind, and anyone would think—seeing that Lucy is the local *femme fatale*, and such a decorative one with that gorgeous hair and the jewels and the supercilious expression, that somewhere in the lady's background there has to be at least an abortion. So why not suggest a live birth? They were all Aunt Sallies, but only a local person could have known their secrets, and their characters. . . .' He was silent, thinking.

'Not Rumney,' she insisted. 'You've got some kind of case, but you have no one to hang it on.'

He said, as if he hadn't heard her: 'Yes, Rumney will do.' He turned his fathomless eyes on her. 'Not a *kind* of case: we've got it all now.'

Chapter 16

CLOUD CAME DOWN and drifted across the moor and the rain started in earnest. It was going to be another wet night. Miss Pink tramped stoically along the path through the heather and in no time she was soaked. She came to the top of Shivery Knott and saw figures toiling up the scree below. Two of them carried a stretcher; several were in dark uniforms. She was far too wet to tolerate delay so she turned aside and descended to the hamlet by way of the wooded slopes at the back of Sandale House.

Grannie Rumney was scraping carrots in the kitchen while Arabella worked through a pile of washing up. At sight of Miss Pink the girl dried her hands and went upstairs to run a bath.

'Where is everyone?' Miss Pink asked, as usual having to shift a comatose cat so that she could sit to unlace her boots.

'They've taken George Harper to the police station,' Grannie told her, 'and there's a crowd of men gone up Shivery Knott with Zeke and some of the Mountain Rescue. I'm sorry that this should have happened: it must have been a shock for you.'

'It wasn't the bodies so much,' Miss Pink said. 'It's the killer's mind.'

'Jackson was led astray,' Grannie said. 'You never could trust him. I didn't say that to Bella because it would have sent her the other way and I thought that, seeing she's a sensible girl, she would find him out before she suffered harm. Bella's got her wits about her, not like that other poor child.'

Arabella came back. She looked pale and subdued.

'Jackson was not the prime mover however,' Miss Pink said.

The girl showed a spark of interest. 'Who was then?'

'I'm not sure. Did the police talk to you?'

'Talk! They're throwing loaded questions about Uncle Zeke! They're mad. They've done nothing yet; you found the bodies, I found Jackson's van—oh, they did find Caroline's Lotus: in a plantation under Whirl Howe. Some forestry workers found it. Her luggage was still inside.'

'I left the money there,' Miss Pink said slowly.

'I know. The police were over there, of course, and the money's gone. What are you puzzling over, Miss Pink?'

'Why was Caroline's car at Whirl Howe?'

'I thought Jackson put it there because he could come home on foot; it's only a short distance back to Sandale over the tops: four miles or so.'

'That would take him no more than an hour and a half. He doesn't appear to have been seen by anyone, which suggests that he didn't get here—or to Shivery Knott—until dusk, just about the time I heard him in the wood.' Absently she started to peel off her wet jersey.

Some time later she knocked on Lucy's back door and waited. She thought she could hear music through the sound of the rising beck. After a moment she depressed the thumblatch, pushed the door—and the final movement of Beethoven's seventh symphony met her, played too loudly. She thought she heard someone singing below the horns, and she stepped round the inner door.

Cole and Lucy faced each other across the room, Cole conducting with large gestures, Lucy in red velvet, sipping tea and regarding him quizzically. When she saw Miss Pink she laughed like a young girl and gestured the older woman to the fire. Miss Pink hung her anorak in the passage. The symphony ended and Cole threw himself on a sofa, red-faced and gasping.

'Come in and have some tea,' Lucy said. 'This man has

176

depraved tastes and thinks Beethoven should assault one's ear drums. He'll be deaf before he's fifty.'

'Such a glorious tone,' Cole enthused. 'I never thought to find a gramophone like this in the sticks—oh, pardon! I'm forgetting my place.'

'Have you been taking your pictures?' Miss Pink asked.

'Not while Beethoven's on, dear.'

A coffee table was loaded with plates of food but Miss Pink declined tea. 'How did your lecture go last night?' she asked, sitting down. Lucy had taken an easy-chair and the firelight played on the red velvet. The only lights were two pale wall-lamps, and the flames flickered over their faces, making a hawk of Cole, an owl of Miss Pink.

'It was interesting,' Lucy said, as if the fact surprised her. 'But what a journey home! There were stones all over the Throat—and the river! It was rather fun though.'

'I know.'

'Of course, you were out last night. Daniel's been telling me. The police were here: asking questions about that wretched letter I had, the anonymous thing. It was a chief inspector who came, a detective; Hendry, is it?'

'Fancy Harper having all that money in his cottage.' Cole's eyes sparkled. 'Did you never suspect?'

'No,' Lucy said. 'How would I?'

'Of course, it was Wren broke in there last Friday,' he said didactically. 'The police told me. Harper's come clean—except that he hasn't said how he got the money.'

'What else has he told them?' Lucy asked.

'Why, all the details of the kidnapping, dear, but then they'll have had most of those from Miss Pink, who would have been more coherent than poor Harper. Wasn't she wonderful, battling through the storm and delivering the money—imagine! She could have been shot!'

'Why?' Lucy asked.

Cole was askance. 'He was there, wasn't he? Hiding in the

177

trees, watching her drop the money, darting out of cover and picking it up, running back to his car, then waiting.'

'What did he wait for?' Miss Pink asked.

'For the other cars to get clear. He couldn't risk his own car being seen in the forest and recognised.'

Lucy lit a cigarette and inhaled deeply. 'Who was it?'

Cole pursed his lips in distaste. 'Zeke.'

Miss Pink gave an angry snort. Lucy stared at the fire. 'Zeke,' she repeated and, as if to herself, 'I've known that man for years.... Do the police suspect him?'

'Oh, yes.'

'The letters—my letter, had to be from a local person; I never thought otherwise.'

Cole looked at Miss Pink. 'That applies to all the blackmail,' she said, 'local knowledge.'

'Starting with Mossop,' Cole continued.

Miss Pink nodded. 'Only someone from the dale could have known about the stolen whisky.'

'Except that it wasn't whisky to begin with,' Cole put in gently. 'It was sheep stealing.'

'So he *was* stealing sheep!' Lucy exclaimed.

'But of course!' Cole became chatty. 'Although the blackmailer didn't know that; all he knew was that he'd seen Mossop's wagon under Whirl Howe, pulling out on the road in the middle of the night, so he rang Mossop saying just that: "What was your wagon doing ... etc?" What a scream!'

Miss Pink smiled. Lucy asked with annoyance, 'What's a scream?'

'He never guessed.'

'About the sheep stealing?'

'No, the sheep was just a bit on the side, a one-off trick; it was too much like hard work and too risky for him to try it twice. No, he never guessed what Mossop's real game was: commuting to the motorway night after night, picking up all the loads falling off backs of lorries all the way from Lancaster to Carlisle. Mossop was terrified.'

'Really?'

'Oh, you'd never have guessed,' he assured her. 'He bluffed. He bluffed the first time the blackmailer rang; he had the feeling, you see, that he was dealing with an amateur—and also the sheep were safely sold and he wasn't going to try that lark again. Well, the blackmailer didn't call his bluff but a few weeks later he phoned again and this time he mentioned stolen whisky. Now the odd thing is that Mossop had none on his premises at that moment, nor anything else that shouldn't have been there, so he told the caller to go to hell. Then they both lay low for a while, until Mossop started to operate again, very cautiously: just one crate of Scotch—and the police were tipped off immediately.' Cole looked straight at Miss Pink.

'Only one person could have known,' she said, watching him. He nodded encouragement. 'Peta,' she murmured.

'That's right: Peta.'

'Well, she was mad,' Lucy said coldly. 'How do you know so much about Mossop's behaviour?'

Cole's eyes opened wide. 'He talked, dear.' He added, placing the words before them like small grenades: 'And then there was Sarah.'

'Sarah?' Lucy seemed bewildered.

'I'm demonstrating why the blackmailer had to be a local,' he said patiently. 'Now Sarah had her accident in September. Did you never wonder,' he asked Miss Pink, 'why Mossop agreed to help her?'

'She paid him.'

Lucy asked, 'When did Sarah have an accident?'

Cole seemed not to hear her but addressed Miss Pink. 'I have a feeling Sarah hasn't told you the truth. After the accident she drove up to Storms but she didn't go to the main building; there's a barn set away from the hotel, and probably she meant to leave her car there and try to see Mossop without anyone else knowing. Of course, she was drunk. And at the barn she ran straight into Mossop, unloading his

179

wagon! It was colour T.V. sets that time. She saw him before he saw her and he hadn't a chance.' Cole looked at Lucy. 'If Mossop had been a killer, Sarah's life wasn't worth much at that moment, but he's a thief, not a murderer, and he struck a bargain: he'd take the damaged car away and get Sarah another one, providing she kept quiet about the load on his wagon.'

'That makes sense,' Miss Pink said, 'but then, someone else had to know.'

'You're suggesting,' Lucy said with interest, 'that Sarah killed the hiker.'

'Yes.' He agreed with both of them. 'Someone noticed that Sarah had a new car and, with the same kind of thought process that had connected crime with Mossop's wagon being on a pass in the middle of the night, connected Sarah's new car with a dead hiker, and this time he hit the target. Sarah paid the first instalment and he knew he'd got her.'

'The devil!' Lucy exclaimed.

'And then there was Peta,' Cole went on. 'I don't know what he found out about Peta. Mossop doesn't know either.'

'It isn't relevant,' Miss Pink said. 'I never met her but she deserves consideration.'

'Yes,' he agreed suddenly, 'she deserved a great deal more than she got.'

Lucy said, 'I'm afraid I had very little sympathy for her.'

'No one seems to have liked her,' he said. 'And yet one doesn't kill people one doesn't like; it has to be something stronger than that—usually.'

'There seem to be two motives involved where Peta was concerned,' Miss Pink mused. 'Money, because she was black-mailed, but then blackmailers don't kill their golden goose.'

'Not normally.' Cole nodded as if she had a good point. 'Do you see a progression here—in violence—and a corre-sponding deterioration in reasoning power? Our black-mailer—' she wished he would not be so familiar, '—starts tentatively with Mossop, and when he won't play, the attempt

180

is abandoned—although he has his revenge by tipping off the police—right?' It was sharp and vulgar and directed at Lucy. Her nostrils flared.

'So you say.'

He turned back to Miss Pink. 'Then he makes a guess with Sarah and it pays off, so he stays with Sarah. Clever not to press it with Mossop, clever to stay with the old lady. But then he starts on a neurotic girl—now that was a mistake—and a girl with no money and that, on the face of it, was stupid, but now listen: Peta had access to money, from the tills and her husband's wallet, but it was terribly dangerous, stealing from her own husband—and such a nasty piece of work as Mossop is. No wonder she nearly went round the bend with worry. I wonder,' he asked of Miss Pink, 'whether that wasn't the idea: to drive her mad—which could be so interesting and so rewarding?'

His listeners were silent and in that silence the telephone rang. Lucy stood up with a polite smile and Cole returned it. She picked up the receiver. 'Hello? Oh, hello, Mark, how nice to hear you. Tonight? No, I'm afraid I've people in. Why, yes, that would be lovely; six o'clock? I'll look forward to it. It *was* rather hairy: rocks on the road and the river nearly over the banks, but I got through without damage. No, not at all, I had a delightful time. Perhaps I should have done that. Tomorrow at six then; goodnight, and thanks for calling.'

'That,' she said, returning to the fire, 'was our speaker from last night suddenly worried, twenty-four hours after the event, that I might not have reached home safely. Not quite twenty-four hours; I left him at eleven. I could have been rolling along the bottom of the lake by now.'

'You came home at eleven,' Cole exclaimed. 'How intrepid you ladies are; it took me all my courage to drive through the Throat in broad daylight.'

'I didn't mean to leave it so late,' she confessed, 'but after the lecture we went to the Saracen's Head and it was closing time before I got away. You know how it is.'

181

'You have great courage,' he insisted. 'All alone in the dark. No wonder you ignored the blackmailer.'

She shrugged. 'You know everything; you must be a detective.'

'Now you're teasing.'

'Don't you think he's a policeman, Miss Pink?'

'He knows a great deal.'

'Ironical,' Lucy said almost idly. 'The people who knew a lot in Sandale died.'

'Well, Peta did,' he conceded. 'You mean Jackson Wren knew too much?'

'Of course.' Lucy turned to the other woman. 'Daniel told me what happened at Shivery Knott.'

'Does he know?' Miss Pink asked innocently.

'Of course—' Cole ignored the question, '—the reason why Wren broke into Harper's cottage the night you gave a party, Lucy, was to steal the money. The person who became the kidnapper was very curious about Harper; as Miss Pink pointed out, Harper was a mystery man, and then he was known to the police. There was that big train robbery last spring and the villains *must* have had inside information. Harper worked on the railways until recently. But the police couldn't get anything on him. However, his friends thought that it would be better for his health if he took a little holiday some distance from the home counties—'

'Although quite near the Glasgow-London line,' murmured Miss Pink, 'where it runs through the wildest country.'

'You have a criminal mind,' Cole told her with disapproval, and continued: 'For one reason and another the local force kept an eye on Harper; they weren't really worried about him, as I see it, but they were interested to see if he had visitors, and who they were. Harper was worried—he has that kind of mind—although not about the police. He was worried about being watched by someone other than the police so, when there was an attempt to break in at Burblethwaite, he changed the locks. To the person who was interested in Harper, when

182

he changed those locks, it was like Sarah paying the first instalment of blackmail money: suspicion was confirmed. Harper had something to hide.'

Miss Pink said, 'I'm surprised *he* wasn't blackmailed.'

'Oh, no; the blackmailer was after bigger game than small instalments; he wanted the lot, if there was a lot. He must have got wind of the police surveillance; that wouldn't be difficult for someone who moved in the right circles. But if Harper had money, he didn't flaunt it, until Caroline turned up, and she spelled money. Wren was sent to Harper's cottage last Friday night to break in and see what he could find, and this time he got in.' He stopped talking.

'Well, what did he find?' Lucy asked.

'Nothing.'

'But the money? It must have been there.'

'Obviously.' He smiled at her.

'So why didn't Wren steal it instead of having to go through all this ghastly business of the kidnapping—and two people being killed?'

'Harper hid the money. You don't think, with one attempted break-in already, and Wren hanging around his cottage, he'd leave fifty thousand lying around?'

Miss Pink asked, frowning, 'Why did you say just now: "the person who *became* the kidnapper"?'

'It was an escalation in violence: attempted blackmail, successful blackmail, murder, but when Wren broke into Harper's cottage, the object was theft. When he couldn't find anything, they put the kidnapping plan into operation, and that was wild. The fellow had gone mad.'

'I don't see that,' Lucy demurred. 'He's got the money; I'd think that meant success, in his terms. Is there something wrong with the money? Is it counterfeit?'

'No, it's almost certainly the proceeds of robberies. The madness lay in the use of an accomplice; that's always risky. And what an accomplice! Of course, he knew that Wren had to be killed eventually, but he'd planned to wait until the crime was completed, the money picked up, stowed away —probably in a Swiss bank—and no suspicion attached to himself. Then he'd kill Wren, simulating an accident. You do realise,' Cole turned to Miss Pink, 'that it could have been just too easy for the kidnapper? Harper would never have asked the police for help, even after he got Caroline back safe, because the money was hot. Oh, yes, it was intended to release Caroline—remember she was bound. After she returned to Harper, the whole thing would have died. The police would have known nothing. Once Wren was killed in an "accident" the kidnapper was as safe as houses.'

'You're playing games,' Lucy said. 'You're making it up as you go along.'

'Like Miss Pink, I have a criminal mind.'

'Like our murderer,' Lucy was sarcastic, imitating his familiarity.

'No, dear; he has no sense of application. He was bound to make mistakes when he got into serious crime. The first was not to move Wren's car.'

'It drew our attention to the locality,' Miss Pink agreed. 'No, that's not quite correct; the fact that it was still here, in Carnthorpe, made me think it would be worth while to question the attendant, and so we learned that Caroline bought boots.'

'Boots,' Lucy repeated, 'what boots?'

'Weren't you told?' Cole asked.

'All that I know about the kidnapping is what you've told me. The police were only interested in the letter I had and whether I'd seen any strangers hanging around at the week-end. Perhaps the bodies hadn't been found when Hendry called on me.'

'That's possible,' Miss Pink said. 'What happened was that Wren wore climbing breeches Saturday morning, which he would hardly do on a trip to London but which he'd wear if he were going climbing, and he took her shopping to buy boots, and all this in full view of the car-park attendant.'

184

'Wren was as thick as two planks,' Cole said. 'Using him was inviting disaster.'

Miss Pink agreed. 'They ought to have gone farther afield or at least left his van where it wouldn't be obvious.' She hesitated. 'And then there was Caroline's car: hidden in the forest certainly but still too close to home. Could the position of the cars have been intended only as a temporary measure?' she asked of Cole. 'There were at least two criminals originally,' she pointed out. 'There could have been a plan for the cars: to take them to Carlisle perhaps, and leave them in a side street with the keys in the ignition so that they would be stolen, or Wren could have been meant to take the Lotus to London to dispose of it.'

'Why didn't it happen like that?' Lucy asked.

'Because Caroline died and Wren panicked. Look at it this way: they went straight to Shivery Knott from Carnthorpe, leaving the Lotus in the scenic park where you left your car today,' Miss Pink told Cole. 'They went to the caves and Wren overpowered Caroline, possibly knocking her out. He tied her up. I wonder if she knew there was a big drop below? I feel she must have been unconscious at some point, and she rolled off the ledge when she started to come round. She would be in pitch darkness, you see.'

'I hadn't thought of that,' Cole said. 'She'd wake up in the dark, would she, and her hands and feet tied? That indicates a certain carelessness on Wren's part. She was also tied to this peg thing?' There was a peculiar lilt in his tone as he addressed Miss Pink.

'Yes, she was tied to the peg by the climbing rope, but he'd left too much slack. If she'd been tight to the peg, she wouldn't have rolled over the edge.'

'Careless,' he repeated thoughtfully. Lucy winced.

'After attacking her and tying her up,' Miss Pink continued, 'he would have driven the Lotus round to the Whirl Howe forest and walked back to Shivery Knott over the tops. I heard him at four o'clock.'

185

'That was when he came out of the cave after discovering Caroline's body,' Cole explained to Lucy.

'Then what happened?' she asked.

'Why, Wren came down and fetched his boss,' he said, 'who went back and shot Wren, almost certainly wiping the gun, and left it there. It wouldn't take long to run up to the crag and back again, would it?'

'He'd do it well inside an hour,' Miss Pink said. 'He didn't have to rig any evidence.'

'Well, of course—' Cole stretched his legs, '—the police will be on to all this.'

'They've started on Arabella,' Miss Pink informed him. 'She was upset.'

A heavy silence descended on the room.

'There are loose ends,' Miss Pink continued after a while. Cole glanced at her ingenuously; he looked tired. Lucy stroked her throat, her rings glittering.

'Harper had the first telephone call, the one saying Caroline was being held, at one o'clock on Saturday. How did Wren communicate with the telephone caller to say that he'd completed the first stage successfully—or was the other criminal in the caves with Wren?'

'No, dear,' Cole said. 'The killer was keeping his hands clean; he was safe in Sandale going about his daily business —except for one quick telephone call to Harper when he knew Caroline had been trapped. Wren had some brilliant clothing and for anyone watching, they'd recognise him on the top of Shivery Knott. He didn't have to signal; his appearance itself was the signal. You can see the whole of the hamlet from the crag.'

'I'm not sure you can see the crag from Sandale House,' Miss Pink put in. 'You can see it from the fields, and most other places on the farm. But going back to mistakes: surely the worst one the killer made was in making further telephone calls to Harper and me yesterday when he'd set up Wren's death to appear as suicide? If Wren were the kidnapper

—people would think—then who made the telephone calls after he was dead? That was the first reason why I thought Wren's death wasn't suicide. And if Wren was murdered it was most likely that he was killed by the person making the telephone calls on Sunday.'

'Why couldn't Wren have made those calls?' Lucy asked.

'Because he was dea—' Miss Pink faltered.

'Yes.' Cole agreed with the unspoken thought. 'We don't *know*. What with the temperature in a cave, and the time of year, and excitement and physical exertion prior to death, it could be difficult to fix when he was killed. I wonder if he could have made those calls yesterday?'

Miss Pink was stubborn. 'If he'd been dead only twelve hours, he should have been partially rigid; besides, it didn't sound in the least like Wren on the phone.'

'People can imitate voices,' he said airily and glanced at Lucy. 'Ah nivver thowt tha wad hev played sic a trick on tha neighbour!' It was a fair imitation of Cumbrian and it startled Miss Pink. Lucy was shocked.

'That's not amusing.'

'It wasn't intended to be; I was demonstrating a point.'

'You're forgetting something,' Miss Pink said. 'In the first telephone call there was heavy traffic in the background.' She looked at Cole. 'Wherever Rumney was, he didn't get to a trunk road at lunch-time Saturday, so who made the one o'clock call, and from where?'

'I expect Zeke's got a gramophone,' Cole said. 'You can buy special effects discs; the radio people use them a lot. Our fellow was clever.'

'You said he was mad,' Lucy reminded him.

'Oh yes, dear, right round the bend. It happens, you know, with these keen minds; they get so sharp they cut their own throats.'

'You mean he'll make a mistake under interrogation?'

'He'll crack; all the mistakes have been made except the last one; the pattern's there, you see; he can't go back.'

187

'But is there any proof?' Lucy asked.

'There are the anonymous letters,' Cole said.

'I burned mine. You mean, the other letters have been found?'

'No, dear, they won't come to light now; they were stolen by the blackmailer and went the way of yours: burned.'

'So they can't be used as evidence; they don't exist.'

'Quite. And the disc with background effects for the phone call: the noise of traffic, that will have been destroyed. But there are two other telephone calls which are quite important.' He said it lightly but Miss Pink stiffened.

'Go on,' Lucy said, 'you're intriguing us.'

'The first telephone call was made the night that the hiker was killed at Storms' bend. It was that call which sent Sarah out on the road drunk.'

'And who made that call?'

'You spoke to Sarah.'

After a moment Lucy said carefully: 'Sarah says I telephoned her on the night the hiker was killed?'

'No. She says she rang you and you said Noble was at Storms.'

'She's a liar.' Lucy was equable. 'What was the second call?'

'That was the night Peta was killed. Someone rang Mossop to tell him that the person who tipped off the police about the stolen whisky in his cellar was Peta.'

Miss Pink gasped. 'It *was* Peta?'

'Indirectly.' Cole was smooth. 'Peta must have known about the whisky and mentioned it in passing to someone close to *her*.'

No one spoke for a moment, then Miss Pink asked: 'What time did Mossop get that call?'

'Some time after half past ten.' Cole didn't look at her but at Lucy. 'At that time Peta was walking from this house to Storms.' He looked round the room as if envisaging her standing in it. 'When she reached the hotel Mossop was waiting for her. There was a violent quarrel. Peta denied

188

tipping off the police, and she was speaking the truth; the tip-off came from the blackmailer. But Mossop was confused and for a moment he thought that Peta herself must have been blackmailing him. He hit her. That was the mark on her face, remember?'

'He killed her,' Lucy said flatly.

'No, dear. He left her where she'd fallen and he went to bed. It's because he's not a killer that he got frightened and eventually he went downstairs to see if she was all right—and found her dead. Now, he knew he hadn't hit her other than on the face; in any case, by now there was a wound as well as a bruise and he knew which he was responsible for, and he knew he'd locked that front door. It was closed, but unlocked. He saw that someone had set it up for him to be the killer, so he removed the body and cleaned up the room. But he knows who killed Peta.'

Only the flames moved among the logs. 'Who?' Lucy asked.

'The person who tipped off the police, who telephoned him, who followed Peta to Storms, who saw her drinking alone through a crack in the curtains, persuaded her to open the door, came in with some excuse for a talk—and killed her.'

'What with?'

'The priest,' Miss Pink said.

'I beg your pardon?' Cole was ritually polite.

'It's hanging above the bar: a lead-weighted weapon like a cosh used for killing salmon. There's blood on it.'

'It ought to be moved,' he said.

'Hendry's taken it,' Miss Pink lied.

'You're suggesting Peta told Denis about the stolen whisky,' Lucy said lightly. 'Fortunately for me, we settled down to television after she went so I couldn't have made the telephone call to Mossop nor followed her to Storms.'

Cole flicked a piece of fluff from his slacks. 'But chaps have to go to the loo, and he doesn't think he watched television. He thinks he went straight to bed. Of course, he admits he was pretty drunk.'

189

'You've questioned everybody.' Miss Pink caught a note of harshness in Lucy's voice and looked up sharply. 'And what was my motive for killing Peta?' The tone was velvety again and Miss Pink lowered her eyes to the other's hands. They were quite still. Absently she wondered how much the rings were worth. She heard Cole saying, 'I don't think it was necessary to kill her—'

But Lucy had stood up. 'Do you want to listen to this?' she asked Miss Pink, 'because I think the evening's entertainment is coming to an end. I have a telephone call to make. Do you mind?'

'Not at all,' Miss Pink said, knowing it was intended as dismissal. She looked at Cole and saw that he was regarding her with cold hatred, then she realised that he was not looking at her, but through her. They sat and waited.

A number was dialled and Miss Pink's ears started to strain as if the telephone were in another room.

'Hello,' Lucy said calmly, 'I've changed my mind; I'll come along tonight after all. They're just leaving; our business didn't take as long as we expected. That will be fine; I'll see you in the bar.'

She came back to the fire. 'He is my alibi for last night; he and about forty-five others. How do you suggest I picked up the money?'

'Lecture halls are dark; I've no doubt you sat by the door.' Cole was bland.

'I can describe the slides and the commentary.'

'Naturally. You talked to the lecturer afterwards, and you'll have discussed the lecture; he sounds the kind of man who could be deceived by a beautiful woman.'

They eyed each other without expression and it was Miss Pink who felt the sweat break out on her skull. The fire was too hot. 'You suggested it wasn't necessary to kill Peta,' she prompted Cole.

'Ah, yes. Murder wasn't the original intention. Peta seduced Denis Noble and Lucy didn't like that—' the other woman

190

made an impatient gesture and he smiled, '—so, guessing—as she'd guessed in Sarah's case, and in Mossop's—she guessed again and started blackmailing the girl.'

'No one guessed,' Miss Pink interrupted. 'The murderer had seen documents relating to Peta's history.'

'Yes?' He looked at her with interest. 'So, ostensibly Peta was blackmailed, but this was only a peg; persecution was the motive. If the girl had another breakdown so much the better. And to help things along she was getting the nasty telephone calls, those where no one said anything. It worked —very well. Noble, like most respectable fools, is terrified of neurotic women, and he returned to the fold. But Peta had been driven too far and although the persecution probably stopped when Noble left her, Peta didn't know it had. Things were still snowballing for her, even if it was only in the mind. She needed help and she made a sudden decision regardless of consequences. She came straight to Noble although he was dining here, but all he could advise was a doctor. However, he meant it and he said that if she didn't go to Bright, he would see the doctor himself on Saturday. Peta had to be stopped from talking and the mind behind it had an outside chance of getting someone else to silence her. That call to Mossop wasn't merely making trouble between husband and wife; it was hoped that Mossop might hit too hard. But, of course, the caller had to follow through and go up to Storms to find out what had happened.'

Miss Pink said, 'Certainly Peta might have told the doctor she was being persecuted but how would that endanger the blackmailer? There was only Peta's word for it—no one else would talk—and the poor girl couldn't have been normal by this time.'

'But it would be out in the open,' Cole insisted. 'Bright might believe her, he might persuade her to go to the police, even to tell Mossop. Then Mossop might, just possibly, admit someone had attempted to blackmail him, pretending that he'd been accused of after-hours drinking parties. Even

Sarah's involvement could be exposed. But do you think the killer used reason? I tell you: the killer was losing control. She had power. She watched Sarah and Peta disintegrate; she saw Mossop, who had defied her, hauled into court. She could terrify people and get money merely by picking up the telephone; she killed Peta and almost pinned the death on Mossop. She enjoyed the plotting, she revelled in the killing.' He turned to Lucy. 'It was exciting, wasn't it?'

'It's made a good story—if in somewhat bad taste, but you're a common little man.' She smiled as if to take the sting out of her words. 'You've got the look of a Baghdad tinker about you. I hope you don't mind my changing my mind about giving you dinner.'

'Not at all,' he said politely.

'You would expect to be poisoned anyway.'

'Oh, no!' He was shocked. 'That's not worthy of you. You've got the vestiges of reason left. Too many people know now. Killing me would be an embarrassment. Miss Pink knows everything. And, put all the bits of stories together: Sarah, Mossop, Harper—the stories the bodies in the caves will tell: you'd have to destroy too much to win now. Where did you get the gun?'

'What gun?'

'They were in Cyprus during the troubles,' Miss Pink said.

'There's no proof of anything,' Lucy reiterated. 'It's just a story.'

'What happened?' he asked. 'Something was missing for you. When were you aware of it and how did you see it: loss of youth and advancing age, the knowledge that life was behind and future existence was all downhill, and drab, and somewhere you'd missed a turning? Were you angry because you'd been a parasite for so long you'd forgotten how to live independently? You had no money, you had to keep Noble. You wanted a new life and security. Life had been sex and affluence but behind it you enjoyed power. When you thought about it you could still have the affluence and power because

192

there was another way of getting them besides sex, and one that meant you didn't have to be an obvious parasite. In fact, you could get your own back at society. You started on crime, carefully at first, but you were successful and the money started to come in—'

'I don't need money,' Lucy said. 'I'm a rich woman.'

'You have this house and you have those rings; what more have you got? There are no more men; even poor old Noble was knocked for six by a neurotic kid, and Noble's in the red anyway. No, dear, it's all behind you, and there was never anything in front either. Turning criminal wasn't the solution for you; you're not criminal calibre. That's a different kind of mind, and not much emotion. Criminals aren't passionate, and they don't make mistakes.'

'There are plenty in prison.'

'Not the successful ones.'

Miss Pink was regarding the other woman fixedly and now Lucy turned to her. 'What do you make of all this?' she asked curiously.

Miss Pink said: 'Odd things have occurred to me. You had an abusive letter, not a blackmailing one. If you'd told Denis Noble that it was blackmail, wouldn't he have insisted on your going to the police, or gone himself? Why were you the person to have the only harmless letter, given your character: a letter that was silly and patently untruthful? It seems that the only similarity between yours and the other letters was that it was anonymous and so, at first sight, you were also a victim.'

'True,' Lucy conceded.

'You went out of your way to stress that you were comfortably off,' Miss Pink went on. 'That was vulgar. You were remarkably indiscreet about your private life. That was undignified. You're neither vulgar nor undignified. You were abnormally excited last Friday night; one wonders why. The impression you gave was of a middle-aged woman infatuated with a younger man, but you're not grieving for Jackson

193

Wren; you've shown no sign of grief at all. Then, on Saturday morning there was a moment when you were overcome by what I thought was the horror of an anonymous letter. You had to have a cigarette and your hands were trembling. Mr Cole suggested that Wren signalled to you when he'd trapped Caroline. Could that have happened at that moment? Your window looks towards Shivery Knott.'

'So it does.' Lucy stood up and Miss Pink followed.

'There is one other thing,' Miss Pink said. 'When Wren discovered Caroline was dead, he ran down here and straight into a house. I heard the door close behind him as I crossed the green. He came to this house.'

'So,' Lucy said, 'I'm a blackmailer and a multiple murderer —if you count Caroline, but where's the proof? What are you going to do about it?'

'Nothing,' Cole said. He motioned Miss Pink before him and they went out to the passage where she collected her anorak and opened the door. He closed it behind them.

Under the gable end she whispered: 'Come up to the Rumneys'.'

'No. Come and sit in my car. It's on the green.'

Chapter 17

THE ASTON MARTIN was parked facing Thornbarrow.

'There isn't a shred of proof,' Miss Pink exclaimed, seating herself in the front and peering through the windscreen.

'There's the money.'

'The fifty thousand?'

'She's got it somewhere.'

'How can we find out?'

'If it's in the house, she won't leave it there when she goes to Carnthorpe, but she could have hidden it somewhere between Whirl Howe and here, to be picked up later.'

'We ought to go to the police.'

'As you say: there's no proof.'

'There's all this fresh information: the telephone call to Mossop after Peta left Thornbarrow—that's damning. What made him tell you about it? He's told no one else—so far as I know.'

'Never mind that now. She may come out at any moment.'

'I'm going to Carnthorpe to find Hendry,' Miss Pink said suddenly. 'If you're right, she'll make a dash for it, and she's mad and very dangerous.'

'It might be an idea.' He was laconic and he yawned without apology.

'*Are* you police, Mr Cole?' He didn't answer. 'If you are,' she continued, 'is there any need for me to go?'

'We could need Hendry,' he murmured. 'What kind of car—? Oh yes, she's got a Jensen Healey.' After a moment he added, very low and as if to himself: 'It would have to be night time.'

'It would have to be,' she repeated aloud, driving down the

195

lane, 'and the floods out again.' And no one left behind in Sandale but Grannie and Arabella, and Daniel Cole watching from the dark car on the green, and Lucy Fell.

She felt stunned. The crimes had been horrible: sadistic, ruthless, inhuman, and yet to suspect an innocent person of them was even more horrible. Miss Pink's mind demanded proof. She would have expected a guilty person to break down, but Cole hadn't broken Lucy. Was her control a sign of guilt? Cole had probed and crowded; his accusations were monstrous if untrue (also if true), yet Lucy stayed cool.

She drove slowly. She wasn't delivering ransom money tonight; Hendry could wait. In any event, he didn't even know that she was coming and, she thought grimly, it was doubtful that he'd believe her. It could sound like some macabre tale told out of school.

The water from the meadows was inching across the road. She rounded Storms' bend, passed High Hollins and Throstle Shaw and her lights illumined the first rock wall. The windscreen wipers clicked away but the rain was easing; it was now the fine drizzle typical of Lakeland. She changed down for the first bend in the gorge.

The river was up and roaring. White water showed in the headlights and she stayed in the middle of the road peering ahead for oncoming traffic.

Where there were fallen rocks last night, there could well be tonight. She thought she must be approaching the place; it was on a straight section, she remembered, not a bend. The wipers scraped the screen, dry, and she switched them off. With perfect visibility she crept round a bend, changed into third, and braked. The road had gone.

She drove forward slowly, still on tarmac but ahead it ran into a sprawled matt mass where points of light winked back at her from stones above the level of the road. It was a landslide.

She stopped and got out. There was no moving this obstruction. Idly, hands in pockets, she walked up to the pile of

196

earth and rocks and broken saplings. It didn't cover the whole of the road; there was a strip of tarmac above the river, but there was no room for a car to get through, not unless one cleared some debris and then drove with both offside wheels canted at a crazy angle. One might do it, with extreme caution, but the river had undermined the bank and on the edge the tarmac was only a crust overhanging the torrent.

She manoeuvred her car to the right-hand verge, not caring if it sank in a ditch, concerned only to get it off the road. She thought she might reverse out of the gorge but then she thought of Lucy driving to Carnthorpe and dismissed the idea. She took a torch from the Austin and locked the doors. She stood beside it, remembering the road through the water-meadows between high walls and with no grass verge and nowhere to go from the path of an advancing car. There was the raised footway, but it was flimsy and could be crashed. As she hesitated, she recalled that the packhorse track ran through the Throat and only about fifty feet above the road. That would be safe.

She shone the torch up the hill past the landslide. There was a fairly easy slope and an outcrop of rock. She started to scramble through the undergrowth, slipping on wet scree and earth. Level with the top of the outcrop she paused and wondered if there were a better route; perhaps she might wait and let Lucy pass. But of course, Lucy couldn't pass. She rested on the outcrop and realised that she was inordinately tired.

Suddenly the Throat was flooded by light as cars came round the bend from Sandale: soundless and very fast. Caught like a moth in the glare Miss Pink watched without conscious thought, only her senses working. She had no time to be aware of anomaly in that the cars were not in line but level with each other, and although she saw the two pairs of head-lights converge and part with an obvious quiver, she was unaware of any significance in the manoeuvre.

Her own dark Austin was revealed in the glare, and the

scream of brakes climbed and held above the roar of the river. The headlights on the inside of the road swung out and those on the river side jibbed in, recovered, and swept past the Austin to cant at an angle as the offside wheels mounted the rubble. It was a sports car, low and sleek and glossy in a normal world, but now vulnerable as a tumbling beetle, rising in terrible slow motion and revealing its underparts, two free wheels spinning in the air like frantic legs. The headlights careened across the gorge, the trees and the low cloud ceiling.

The roof hit the water first and there was no splash to speak of. The car didn't sink immediately but was carried in the foam for some distance, the lights shining through the waves until their gold faded to white and then went out suddenly and there was nothing but the river raging through the Throat.

The scene was still lit. Miss Pink brought her aching gaze back to the landslide before which the second car stood with its headlights blazing. Daniel Cole was on the tarmac staring at the river. She scrambled down to the road and at last he turned and walked towards her.

'She had the money,' he said.

'How did you know it was the money?'

They had reversed their cars and turned, and were sitting in Miss Pink's Austin at the foot of the doctor's drive.

'If she made a break for it, wasn't she the killer?'

'You know damn well she wasn't, necessarily.' She was suffering from shock. 'There was no proof. She could have been upset or frightened by your questions and decided to go away for a while.' There was a pause. 'She didn't appear to be frightened,' she added with fairness.

'She wasn't.'

'You pushed her.'

'I was pushing all the time: trying to make her crack.'

'I mean: in the gorge. You were bumping her as you came down the straight towards the landslide. I saw her headlights jerk as the cars touched. There will be marks on your nearside wing.'

'I tried to block her as she left the hamlet but she managed to scrape past. As for her guilt: when her car is lifted, they'll find the money.'

'How did you know she was carrying it?'

'What will you tell the police?'

'What will *you* tell them?'

'That I suspected she was the killer, that you drove away to Carnthorpe to alert Hendry while I watched to see if she'd make a break for it. When she did, I tried to stop her, but she got away and I followed.'

'Will you say how close you were to her in the Throat?'

'No. And I don't think that you will.'

'Is that a threat?'

In the growing light his head turned towards her. He said quietly: 'You mustn't forget Caroline: regaining consciousness in the dark and her hands and feet tied. How long do you think it took for her to die?'

She watched the light intensify over the Central Fells and wondered if anyone were up there at this moment, alone and alive.

'I'll tell the same story,' she said, 'at least until they raise the car.'

'And when they find that the money's there?'

'I'll stick to the story. But you must tell me how you knew she had the money.'

'I didn't know until she tried to escape, and then I put my headlights on and recognised the case. I bought it in the leather market in Istanbul.'

'It was George Harper's case!'

'Poor old George.' There was a smile in his voice. 'He couldn't have raised five thousand, let alone fifty. He's broke.'

Miss Pink asked weakly, knowing the answer: 'How did he get it?'

'I brought it from London, dear: Saturday afternoon, after I had his phone call.'

The moon sailed clear and the meadows were flooded with quicksilver. 'The money didn't mean much to me,' Cole was saying apologetically, 'except as an instrument to save Caroline—and I owed George a favour or two. I happened to have a bit to spare.'

'Fifty thousand!'

He coughed deprecatingly. 'Well, it's only money, isn't it?'

'So you knew Harper.'

'Quite well; he's a friend of mine. And Caroline, of course. I was fond of Caroline.'

'Why didn't Harper tell me? How could he succeed in keeping it from me? He was at his wits' end while we waited to see if the money had been picked up.'

'Yes, but he was frantic because he knew the money had gone and yet they hadn't released Caroline.'

'But no one knew the money had gone until today!'

'George knew before you got back to Sandale last night— because I was at the drop. I waited at Storms earlier in the evening and George rang me after you left for Whirl Howe. I was in one of the cars coming up the road when you came out of the forest after dropping the money. You saved me some time by showing me which entrance to use but even then, when I reached the place the money was gone. As I said at Thornbarrow: she must have darted out of the trees where she was waiting and picked it up immediately you'd put it down by those beater things. She'd have worked out in advance where to leave her car so that it would be hidden but wouldn't get stuck in the mud. I didn't look for a car once I found the money was gone; I reckoned whoever picked up the case hadn't hung around. I got back to the road and streaked into Carnthorpe but the only car I passed that meant anything to me was yours. I'm surprised she could drive so well although—' he added darkly, '—she wasn't all that good tonight.' Miss Pink thought that he had the landslide to thank

200

for that but she didn't interrupt. 'Remember,' he went on, 'I wasn't sure who I was after last night, and when I reached Carnthorpe I knew that the chap I was chasing could have gone towards the motorway or to Carlisle or back to Sandale. I reckoned it was a Sandale resident because of the old black-mailing business and I thought that person wouldn't want to be absent from home, or appearing to be absent, at the time the money was picked up.

'I stopped in Carnthorpe and rang George to tell him that the money was gone and not to tell you because you'd have wanted to know how he knew. Then I raced up to Storms and started phoning the Sandale people to find out where they were. That was the advantage of being Press; I didn't need, a pretext for talking to people. The only ones absent were Rumney and Lucy.'

'Is that why you suspected him? He'd be out looking at his cows.'

'I never suspected him; I used him as a red herring. If I could make you think he was a suspect, I might use him as a decoy with the criminal. Not that I really needed him; by the time I came to Lucy I was almost sure. This morning I went to look at the hall where the lecture was held; it's near the main car park and she could have slipped out easily in the dark.'

'And the telephone call to me at seven-thirty?'

'The lecture started at a quarter to eight—and there are two kiosks in the market square.'

'I'm surprised that Harper didn't tell me he knew you; I thought I had his confidence.'

'I didn't want a tie-up with George; the police might have become more interested in me than in Caroline. After all, she's only a villain's daughter to them. Besides, who trusts them? You can always do the job better yourself. Another thing: we played along with the kidnapper not to bring in the authorities or any honest citizens barring yourself, but I was different. I went to the forest to catch the one who picked up the money and if I'd got him, he'd have talked.' There was a pause. 'Even when I found who it was,' he added.

'And I thought you were a crime reporter—even someone from Scotland Yard at one time.'

'But I really am a journalist; I do feature articles for abroad. I just played myself—well, a facet of myself; even on a conservation story I could poke around and ask all the indiscreet questions which the public thinks the Press has a licence to ask. I went all over Thornbarrow and, although Lucy ticked me off for mentioning Jackson Wren, she had to retract. I was too dangerous and she had too much to hide.'

'Did you tell Mossop that you were—something more than a reporter?'

'Not exactly; he has the impression that I'm one of his employers—he didn't work on his own, of course—one of the big men come down from the Smoke to see what he's been up to. That's why he came clean. You see, I was in touch with George before ever I arrived so I knew that Mossop had just been caught for receiving, and George said he was a villain. So I knew what I had to deal with and it was a big break for me; he was useful, he knew a whole side of Sandale that George didn't—the blackmailing, for instance. He got the impression that I thought he'd killed his wife and that we were annoyed because he'd attracted attention to the hotel. To protect himself he told me everything he knew about the locals, and he told me what he did when he found Peta dead, and about that telephone call saying she had tipped off the police. He guessed that the caller killed Peta but he wasn't in a position to do anything about it. He was afraid of the big boys, you see, if he didn't keep a low profile.'

'I see why he was so frightened yesterday morning; Rumney thought he was worried because we'd turned up to accuse him of stealing sheep.'

'He was right, in a sense. I'd given Mossop a hearing over the affair of his wife and I'd allowed him to assume that he'd

202

convinced me he hadn't killed her and that he hadn't been responsible for all the police activity afterwards, just unlucky. I hadn't let him off the hook though because he was more useful to me while I had a good hold on him, but he thought he might be in the clear if he behaved himself and did as he was told. Then you come in and accuse him of stealing sheep —and he was supposed to be working for *us*, not running his own little side-lines!'

'Are you associated with the people employing him, Mr Cole?'

'Oh no, dear!' He was shocked. 'Heaven forbid! They're East End boys!'

'What do you deal in?'

'We're going to get into hot water with that nice chief inspector if we don't report the accident. Oh hell, think of all the questions they're going to ask! Let's go up to Storms and fortify ourselves and start telephoning. We've got a busy night ahead.'

When the level of the river went down, the Jensen was raised and inside it they found, beside the drowned body of Lucy Fell, a suitcase containing fifty thousand pounds in used bank-notes. Harper said that the money had been lent to him by Daniel Cole, but Mr Cole was unable to confirm this because he was not available. However, Miss Pink corroborated the story but she was unable to say anything about Mr Cole's activities other than that she understood him to be a journalist.

The inquest on Peta Mossop was resumed and the verdict on both her and Jackson Wren was murder by Lucy Fell; that on Caroline and Lucy Fell was misadventure, which had a peculiar appositeness.

Sarah was a casualty; she got two years but, as she wrote to Miss Pink, time was relative and those two years could not be as bad nor as long as the weeks since she'd killed the hiker.

No one chased Mossop, who put Storms up for sale and went to Newcastle.

203

Harper gave up the lease of Burblethwaite. Daniel S. Cole had disappeared as soon as the Throat was passable, leaving behind a fortune in hot money, a suitcase from Istanbul and a visiting card—which was genuine, but the David Ramet Institute of Environmental Studies and the Hampstead address never saw him again. He vanished in the Smoke.